THe OATh-TaKERS

Naomi Mitchison was born in 1897 in Edinburgh, the daughter of eminent scientist J.S. Haldane, and educated at Oxford. For the past seventy years she has been regarded as one of the leading historical novelists of her generation, with her careful research and imaginative gift. Her marriage to politician Dick Mitchison in 1916 led to her own involvement in a social and political context in London and then in Argyll, where she returned to live in 1937. She has had over seventy books published, including biograhies, short stories and poetry, and her numerous historical novels include *The Corn King and the Spring Queen, Blood of the Martyrs,* and *The Bull Calves.* She lives in Argyll as well as in London.

The OATH-TAKERS

Naomi Mitchison

WITH ILLUSTRATIONS BY
BARBARA ROBERTSON

BALNAIN BOOKS

Back cover photograph of the author by Sally Mitchison

Printed and bound in Britain by BPCC Wheatons of Exeter
Covers printed by Wood Westworth, St Helens.

Published in 1991
by Balnain Books,
Druim House, Lochloy Road,
Nairn IV12 5LF
Scotland

The publisher gratefully acknowledge subsidy from the Scottish
Arts Council towards the publication of this volume

British Library Cataloguing in Publication Data:
Mitchison, Naomi 1897-
    The Oath-Takers.
    1. Title
    823.912 [F]

ISBN 1 872557 03 1

LOOKING back on European history, we begin to see a pattern: the sheets of this history separate and turn over, no doubt squashing a great many nameless and a few named people in the process. And then? It is different for the genuine, professional hunter, but for most of us, dipping back to school days, there is often a single person who stands out, like a full-page advertisement for his or her period. This gets more difficult to pick out in the last couple of centuries, let alone overcrowded now. Of course, for a real historian this is nonsense, but it is how things look for story-tellers like myself.

These turn-over points are very fascinating. What is underneath? What is about to show? Is this little green seedling going to turn into an oak tree or is it a weed to be pulled out and thrown away as soon as possible? We story-tellers have a delightful time playing with history, perhaps finding something fascinating, perhaps making dreadful mistakes.

There are quite hard rules to the history fiction game. We have to think out what is really important in the new picture after the turn-over. Has the historical 'big print' happening changed life among the un-named mass of common people and, if it has, were they aware of it or did they think it would blow away? And, all the time for the fiction writer, the whisper: what kind of story could this make? What kind of people would, at a given period of social and political change, be most involved and so most likely to make a good story?

Given time, the story-teller sorts out the history, so that, at least, there is a fairly accurate look around at the world — not of course the whole world, not Europe, not some part of the Mediterranean culture, not even one small kingdom — but a few individuals together for some purpose: defence, food, religion. Well then, the thing begins to take solidity. Out of the historical situation come the possible relations between people, and then the people themselves, the individuals who are to be the story.

This is an exciting time for the writer. Who will be the main character? Male or female? If females, then the story, the view, may have to be limited and even impossible, unless the society and date which has been chosen allows women a reasonably wide possibility of life and decisions, which can be turned into a real what-happens-next story. There is much more freedom of action for the male, just as, in my school days, the boys' magazines were so much more fun than the girls'. It's as simple as that.

So, the story-teller begins to get the feeling that hereabout in history there is the time and place that fits: the changes, the temptations, the joys and hurts, above all how someone in the chosen period looks at and assesses the world around and beyond. How is he or she likely to act? ...And then the writing. Most likely the story-teller goes far from the original story. Things turn up. Real people, about whom something is known, turn up but with luck he or she is looked at from a new point of view. Others turn up, apparently by accident. Part of the fun for the story-teller is to introduce something new but plausible, and stand back. And of course, the better the story, the more it insists on telling itself, and on bringing in unexpected new people and places.

This happens all the more when the story-teller decides on a period when history is turning over, new ideas coming in, old habits losing their grip, having to change.

So, to come to this book which I hope you are going to read... when I was shuffling around in bits of history, it began to look to me that Charlemagne was going to be the central maypole round which the people of this story, set in mid-Europe, must swing and fall. Whether he was alive or dead he would remain a central figure. As I began to look more closely, it also seemed as though here was the beginning of the social attitude and expected action which we call feudalism.

It was also clear that the Church, whatever it looked like, was the one place where certain important aspects of morality, and decent conventional living as well, were to some extent kept alive. Almost every written or legal word was in Latin and all education was in Church hands, including Latin grammar and the ability of the educated to read and write in Latin. While I was still writing this book, something came up at a prestigious auction sale: a boy's Latin grammar book of the date which I had fixed on, given to him by his mother and with a few school blots and giggles. Solid evidence: always a pleasure. I wish I could have seen it.

9

So here was the network of history, the pegging down of dates. I wrote and wrote and the people became alive and the story twisted and elaborated under my eyes and I felt my people's moral and family diversities and I saw ahead of them, but sometimes allowed them to escape some particular difficulty. But there was always the question — have I got it right? Were they really like that? Probably not. Then I got the essential book which had the history I was clinging onto; now I need no longer be lost in a tangle of dates and deep uncertainties. For this story it was *The Frankish Kingdoms* by Rosalind MacKitterick. Here was the world whose gates I had been crawling round and sniffing at. Then there was *The Carolingians and the Written Word*. Above all here was their writer and it appeared that, unlike some other historians, she was someone who would answer even one's silliest questions. Now that this bit of the past was firmly at the back door, I could dash in any moment and steal an apple!

So much for the adventures coming to the young man which, I hope, you will be reading about now.

PART ONE

I SCARCELY knew my father. How could it be

otherwise? My true fathers were back in the Abbey, gravely about their business, but loving me. This other was at the far side of the table behind the great lights and the noises of food and drink and always a great buzzing of people, fawning to him, listening to him speak — and it could be a great shouting and frightened faces. Beside him but not with him my mother whom I  hardly knew, though I wished to, sitting like a statue, like Our Lady herself, in a glitter of gold and red. There would always be some from the wide-stretched family of which we were all part, uncles, cousins, some old and difficult. We had married into families like ourselves, sometimes up, sometimes, perhaps, down. All of them must be hospitably entertained, as they in turn, would do by us.

I remember my aunt Adelheid, whom we often saw, because she was the Abbess of a small community fairly near. I hoped she might be moved to speak to me about holy things, but no, it seemed to be always about the Abbey's farm land, inherited from the first founder, how to deal with the serfs, whether she should shift the cropping this way or that, seldom on what, surely, must be where her real thoughts and problems lay. But it was not my place to speak.

The older uncles would thump the table and shout at my father, but, family-wise, he made the big decisions. If there were punishments, they were in his hands, though his old cousin, who held the great meadow in the crook of our small river and also the south slope with the vines, and who was always spitting on the floor, had to have his say. So did another of my aunts who had married in from a greater family; she had a small squeaking dog, which she fed at table with scraps. I think the real dogs, our hunting dogs, hated it jealously.

They all could be at top pitch and banging on the table. Sometimes I would be scared that I would be called on and must leap up putting on a smile, perhaps to carry a cup or a plate of meat, and always to face rough talk, joking I did not want to understand, songs that seemed to batter against all I had learned, and tried to break into me. How glad I would be when it finished and I could take myself out of sight and sound, past the dark end of the hall where the slaves and the hounds were going through any thrown-out bits of meat. Often that meant among the horses; for at least my father had given orders that I should have the best and my own little horse, Suelde, was all of that. Whatever we say about the Saracens and we know that they are damned, it would be a great lie to say anything but good of their horses.

After the banquet and the noise and the smell of beer or, at the top table, wine, and also of meat and vomit, it was so good to get back to the quiet and the controlled voices and the knowledge of my other fathers and teachers. Even when I was on my horse, I could hear their voices inside my head, not shouting but telling me true things, making me understand deeply that I was part of something almost as great as the heavens themselves, the Empire of God, of Rome, under the protection of an anointed King. I could think of that and it became a great comfort and I could excuse the shouting and battering that my father seemed part of, because he was, in the final sense, a Roman. We Franks are all Romans, knowing that our Empire is the truth.

My Abbot, who told me everything, had made me aware of how we ourselves were the protectors of the Christian world and that was the meaning of the great oaths which were taken by our King and Emperor. This was why the King's promise had been made and was valid to all his subjects, of whom the great ones to whom he had given land and power, made the same oath to him.

I had been taught to read and write a little, yet this might not have happened, but that the Great Charles ordered that the sons of Lords must get this training, raising themselves into true citizens. I had two kinds of speech in my head. One was the noble speech, Latin, in which I moved, mind and tongue, when I was at home in the Abbey with my friends and teachers and fellow pupils. The other was the common speech, Frankish, which I spoke in the Hall or to the servants and women and grooms.

I used the noble speech with my father, but sometimes he would break off into Frankish if one of his old fighters came up to him. He too had been taught by the Benedictines, but he had forgotten much. I always tried the noble language, not only on my mother, who knew a little, but on my young brothers, though Ulric only laughed at me, and the little one, Malfrid, used to run off a string of Latin words just for the fun of it. So did my half brother, whose mother I was told not to look at. But I liked Haimo and he liked me, although he was a little frightened of me, because I could read and write my name in Latin, and also, I suppose, because one day I would be his lord.

I love to think about the Abbey. There were so many stories inside the walls, inside the thinking of our teachers and fathers. First there were the stories out of Holy Writ and the many stories of the lives and sufferings of the saints and martyrs, more than all the stars in the sky. And there were stories of the great Romans, of Caesar, Scipio and Cicero and of the great clerics and founders of Abbeys and Orders, like a vast array of warriors, armed and ready. They formed a part of our army in the world battle that was forever happening between good and bad, with the false Emperor of the East who lived in wicked Byzantium in a palace of gold and blood and women, attempting all the time to undermine and get possession of our true Roman Empire of which we Franks are the only, because the bravest, protectors. Above all there were the stories of our own Frankish heroes.

Even as a child my heart went out to our great Christian king who, with his warrior lords, had beaten back the heathen Saracens at Roncesvalles, although at such great loss. I remember weeping when I understood that this was many years back and the great Charles was dead, as dead as Roland of the Marches. Yet he had left a son Louis who was the anointed Emperor and he in turn had left sons who were kings and had taken the great oaths as guardians of Christendom, though surely only one could be the greatest. Or had I understood it wrongly? There were puzzles... My teachers seemed unwilling to tell me plainly whom I should consider as my true King to whom I would owe service when I was older.

Then there were other stories of different fighting and a different kind of courage from that of the martyrs. These were the doings of the Franks before they had been led into Christianity and at first I was afraid that, although they were so brave, they must have missed heaven. Yet they were not in hell since they were our father's fathers who had brought the first Hludovic to save the Empire from ruin and heresy. I did not altogether understand heresy, but I knew that it was bad and a trap for believers. As well as that they had killed wolves and bears and cleared the world of dragons which used to fly and creep and make havoc everywhere. One of my teachers was adept at drawing dragons, though he himself

17

had never seen one.

Sometimes I was taken to see my father doing justice and sometimes my brother Ulric came as well. One of my teachers from the Abbey would come with me and explain, since, in a sense, my father was doing God's work, because most of those whom he was judging had broken one Commandment or another. My teachers would point this out, but there was little of Holy Writ in what was said: indeed it seemed to me to go back, often enough, to early days before we Franks had seen the light, before Roman law, when we were truly barbarians.

Most of the cases that came before my father were quarrels, wounding, house-breaking, driving of another's cattle, rape of a daughter, or what would you, and mostly the whole families involved and their neighbours, threatening and crying and cutting across one another. All these would be men sworn to my father, Free Franks. But my father could and did stop all this noise; he called witnesses, put questions and listened.

It was the same in the quarrels about inheritance, and perhaps all of a family or all of a village shrieking and baying about what their grandparents had promised but not put into writing since they could not write. How glad I felt of my education! Yet I knew that these people were good underneath, were fellow Franks.

Then there were killings: women in tears with blood-clotted clothes. These were mostly at the bad end of a quarrel about property. A strip of land, a cow, an old coat, anything might lead to a fight and sometimes onlookers brought in, taking sides, one thing leading to another, everyone in confusion and wanting it not to have happened, and my father having to sort it all out. He shouted at them, which I did not like, but they expected.

He did all this well enough and it could even be a relief to the man who had done grievous wrong to be shouted at, treated like a bad child. If it was all plain, the man who had done the killing or his family would have the money ready or promised to the kin of the dead man or woman, though some gold would go to my father to pay for his trouble and justice; he said to me that it went on to the King whom he represented.

Sometimes it was not all straight-forward and my father might hold the suspect locked up, or else a man might be accused but swore he was innocent and would ask to take the ordeal. That was always very exciting, but often it seemed not to happen. Older people would get together and something would be agreed on, though I always hoped I would one day see an innocent man pick up a red-hot bar without even a blister on his hands.

I do not know if this was Roman law, perhaps not. We Franks want to keep our own laws, handed down from far back but constantly cleaned and polished by the great thoughts of the Christian world. That is how things should be. My teachers had many examples of crimes which men and women might commit, and what punishments were due.

But do not think I was only listening and learning. For I was learning many other things. My father, or one of my kin, or old Walakind, would take me riding in the forest or up into the hills to the East. I knew much beauty and bird songs that put me in mind of the stories in which young heroes were guided by forest birds to great adventures. I learned to hunt with bow and arrow or with boar spear. I knew the names of all the hounds. This was rough teaching and my father was in a quick anger if I missed or if he thought I was afraid, even if I was not.

I liked most to be out and doing the things of manhood, yet I knew that the other teaching was also necessary. But I did not like working alone in my cell at the Abbey, with only a small lamp, unless I was allowed to take with me one of the beautiful books from the library. It might be the life of one of the saints, or, as I began to find Latin easier to read, it could be Prudentius, or a very old poem by Virgil that was difficult to understand but sounded beautiful when I said it to myself. Or sometimes they let me have one of the illustrated psalters, with pictures like bright gateways into another world.

I fell in love, as one might say, with St. Mark's lion. I could have held that little lion in my arms! These books wrapped me round with words and colours, but without them sometimes I dreamed of devils. This was bad, for they could be coming into my mind, even in broad daylight, so that they appeared and spoke to me. But not when I could look up to the high roof of the Abbey, pointing skywards, only in the wild forest.

Just once, I spoke of this to my mother, but she said, No, no, it was wrong to be frightened of such things. I was old enough to understand that fear was not for men. And then she told me that soon my father must go and take oaths and perhaps I could ride with him to the great city and perhaps set eyes on the anointed one, the Emperor. So I was most careful that all should go well, that nobody could find fault with me.

Then my older sister, Hiltrud, gave me a precious thing which would keep the devils away. Our mother must have spoken to her of what I had said, so here was a little cross made of a kind of thin, brittle wood and tied with gold wire. It had come from far away, she said, and carried blessing. I must wear it next to my heart. I was sorry for Hiltrud because she was to be married to a lord from three days ride south and west, and although she liked the bride-price jewels he brought for her when he came to our father to bargain for her, she had not liked either the look of him or the kiss he gave with the jewels. But it was all settled over her head. She had no choice.

None of us have much choice. When my father sent word to the Abbey that I must ride with him and that I too must take the oath, nobody asked did I want to go. But I did want, so that his will and God's will and my own will went together. The best thing was that my father ordered that my half brother Haimo should come to wait on me. He was the same age as I was. Sometimes I thought of my father going from the noble bed of my mother, having got me on her, and perhaps drinking and warming himself again before going to the haybed of Haimo's mother who perhaps had not expected him, perhaps was deep afraid.

When I am only a little older, I thought, all this will become easier to see. Yes, I too. But other times I thought, Should I become a saint and throw such thoughts away, allowing women only to kiss my feet? But I had not let such thoughts go further than my teeth. As I waited for my father to come to a decision I wondered about the oaths and worked myself into headaches thinking about what they might be, and at last, on the day before I left, I begged permission to ask the Abbot.

That was always something very grave. The teaching Benedictines are strict and need to be; I have been whacked often and mostly I deserved it, though sometimes not. The Abbot would never lay a hand on boy or man, but his look could make one shiver; it was certain that he was directly under God. He told me what I knew already, that we Franks are the true guardians of the Christian world, the Empire that came to birth long ago when Saint Peter and Saint Paul came to Rome, bringing the doctrine to that part of the wide world where it has stayed and grown. What he planted was watered by the blood of the first martyrs. Before that, there was ignorance and a great void, yet heaven's gate was not totally closed, for those such as our own heathen Frankish ancestors might still be saved through innate virtue. But once the Church, being the temporal Empire, had come into being, ignorance was no excuse. Hell was waiting to catch with pitchforks those who slipped, who were not indentured to Goodness.

So the oath which had first been taken by the anointed Emperor — the great Charles himself — kneeling before the Pope, father of us all, was of deep importance, since on taking it, he at once became the key to heaven's gate and the caster of this great net which encloses all Christendom. In turn, the oath of those whom he had chosen as his first comrades and helpers was a deep thing, for it was given in the presence and the touch of God's anointed, as though in the presence of God. The chosen ones, in turn, were leaders of the great army of Imperial Christendom; they laid down their lives as the Franks have always willingly done in battle for their commanders. They held the frontiers against the heathen Saxons and Avars in the east and the Saracens in the west. Yes, all of that I knew and understood, how they had done this in obedience to their oaths.

My lord Abbot spoke of all this while I listened at his feet, about how the key to the Empire of the Franks, the protectors of Christendom, had been passed on from the Great Charles to his son Louis — called the Pious, and for good reason, said my Abbot, since he had done great things for the Bishops and the monasteries — and then to a new and young Charles, who might yet become the mirror of his grandfather. He had his enemies and it appeared, sadly, that his brothers were jealous of him, but he had shown great piety. An oath to him would be as binding as that to the great Charles to whom my grandfather had given his oath.

"You should know, my child," said the Abbot, "that your father had been summoned before this to take the oath, but there was yet another bitter war, so your father and his men were sent to that and the time for the oath passed by. That was when your father's young brother was killed — the uncle you should remember for he was always giving you sweetmeats and nuts -"

Yes, I remembered him, his red beard and blue eyes and he never came back.

"So now," said my Abbot, "your father must give

his oath to the Count of Paris who stands as deputy to the Anointed King and who will put his name into writing and send it to the great Royal Chancery." He stopped for a moment, and then went on, more gravely: "My hope is that the Young King has not given over-much power to the Counts and Margraves. That could do harm to Christendom." And then he spoke of Roncesvalles and of many Christian battles and of the founding of monasteries and works of courage and virtue, all following from the oaths which had been taken and were forever urging the takers into noble deeds. My ears rang with the great names.

It was in a way hard for me to think of my own father, going to take a sacred oath, as the kind of hero who could match the Abbot's talk. Yet maybe, when the time came, his name too might come into the hero songs, his soul, purified, into the congregations of heaven. And I myself, if God and my luck were true to me, I also could be there!

SO IT WAS

that there was much in my mind when we started one morning of early summer. I had ridden before with my father to the May-day meeting of the fighting men from many parts of the kingdom with all their gear and all their songs, controlled by their lords, but only just. There had been noise all the time, shrieking or blasting trumpets, battering and clattering of sticks and swords on shields, high whinnying of war horses.

It was different this time. We moved faster, south and west, and my father was not jolly or easy, spoke little and not to me.

"Better keep out of sight," Haimo whispered, as

we took our bits of half-cooked meat to chew on while the men dragged big logs of fallen timber onto the fire.

I asked Haimo why he thought this.

"He is afraid of the oath taking," said Haimo, and then laughed. "You too will be afraid when it is your turn."

I chewed that over in my mind, for at first I was angry. I thought fealty to a King, an anointed King, that means something directly from God. And, even if it is not the direct oath, but through another channel, as wine is poured from the vat into a jug before the cup. Then I thought of Roncesvalles. The great Charles was dead, but all had been passed on. The Empire *was* safe.

It was slow going through the forest. The paths were not wide enough for a waggon, so that we had to take pack-horses. I knew that some of them had gifts they were carrying, others had clothes and footgear of a kind to be worn in presence of the great. Some had iron armour and a few mail shirts; then there were our day to day provisions and my father's heavy travelling chair for him to rest in. He kept his dagger by his side as we all did, and also his hammer-axe, but felt safe enough to leave his heavy sword and shield for the horses to carry. We all kept our hunting bows ready; in some parts of the forest there were plenty of chances for a shot.

There were streams to cross, the horses to be gentled through water and sticky mud. I waded, leading my Suelde, the saddle cloths pulled up so that at least I would get a dry seat at the end, and my own hose and short boots piled on my head, and also my beautiful prayer book, fine vellum with the capitals coloured, given me by my Abbot. Afterwards the older men, especially old Walakind, would help me and show me how to dry off my bow and my dagger on moss and leaves. But it seemed that much of this was on purpose to harden me, and also of course, Haimo. I was very willing to be hardened and I made pictures in my mind of the anointed King whom I might see face to face. Would that be a thing to fear, or would I be overwhelmed by some kind of love? I did not know. But the right words, even the right looks, would surely be told to me.

Then there came a great, bright river, lying across our way, with a boat and tough ferry men asking and getting gold pay. Some of the horses had to swim, pulled behind the ferry boat, but my father's great horse, which was worth many men, and my Suelde and Haimo's horse which was from the same mare as mine, were led onto the strong timbers of the ferry boat. We stood beside them and spoke to them to stop them being afraid.

At the far side were better paths and more crop fields and people to be seen. I asked if we were now near to the place of the oath taking but the men were uncertain, even Walakind. He was Haimo's uncle, the oldest and best thought of among the free men, someone with cattle and sheep and a good strip of ploughland and forest. This of course he held from my father, but it was his own to do with what he liked.

I did not like to ask a direct question of my father. It might have angered him. Then came more cleared land, cattle, horses, thatched huts and then a small stone church, but we did not stop. There were more people, horsemen, monks and nuns, sellers of all kinds of things, armed parties who stopped us and then waved us on. But my father was not talking to me. He was becoming less like himself, less sure. He was angry at small things, as if he hated us all.

"It is because of the oath," said Walakind. "It is a sore thing. A man cannot be altogether free when he has taken a great oath."

"As one is tied by baptism," said Haimo.

But I was puzzled. "If one is not baptised," I said, "Hell is open. When we are baptised, we make our escape from hell. We are free. We have said No to Satan."

"Maybe," said Haimo, "but it is worse if we slip. It is the same with a great oath. If a man breaks that, or even thinks of breaking it, he is in deep water."

"Yes" said old Walakind. "You boys keep away from oath taking."

Then I remembered what the Abbot had said once. I had not thought about it much at the time, but I did now. When it came to the time when the Great Charles took the enormous oath of Emperor, he sent out his letters of demand to all his subjects and the clergy most of all, making strict rules of order, obedience, chastity, all within a new oath of fidelity to himself. For now he had become deeply other than he had been, because from King he had become Emperor, the governor of the Roman Empire as well as his own domains, most of all his ancient Frankish kingdom. So his subjects must remain always true to God, which means justice for all, even women, even strangers, or slaves who must not be sold out of Christendom.

It is said — and this my Abbot told me — that

even Charles was reluctant to take this great and terrifying oath, thinking it was perhaps beyond mortal grasp. It could be that a King might fear God's judgement on himself if, in spite of orders, those he ruled were doing evil. So I thought I could understand why my father was taking things so ill, and felt sorry for him, if a boy can ever be truly sorry for a grown man.

Although we were now within the boundaries of the Count's land, it was another full day's journey before we reached the Seine river which we must follow until we came to Paris itself, standing, as I had been told, on a guarded island. Now we found ourselves coming in sight of a small castle, moated round and with a guarded gate. However, after some trouble and sending of messages, the gate was opened for us and we were welcomed, though not very heartily. Indeed it was a sad place, for the old lord who lived there had lost his eldest son in a skirmish, which he seemed to blame sometimes on King Lothar and sometimes on King Charles. Another son had died and he spoke darkly about witchcraft, so that we all felt uneasy.

There was a room in the tower for my father and me, but Haimo stayed with his uncle and the horses. Walakind, I know, kept himself armed, because of the good things the horses were carrying. Haimo carried up my father's travelling chair, which he could sleep in more soundly than on the hay and sheep skins which had been brought for us. I was full of flea and bug bites by morning. So it was no cheerful place we were in.

I kept to a corner of the room, where there was a slit window, but my father suddenly called me over.

I had not expected it. He was sitting there in his leather travelling chair like a bear in a hollow tree and said, growling, "Do you know what an oath is?"

It surprised me that he wanted to speak with me, but I felt I must answer in a serious and courteous way.

"I believe I do, my Lord Father," I said. "It is to be faithful, as a man rightly should be to his lord. And I understand that I must take it beside you."

He seemed to chew on his words, almost biting them, then he said, "I am angry. But I am not angry with you." So I breathed again. He went on, "But consider: who is this Lord?"

"Surely, the crowned King of the Franks — it is to him we are going?" For that was what I had in my mind.

"No!" said my father. "Maybe I — we — shall see him one day. Maybe not. We go to the Count of Paris. He passes on the oaths: our names, written down. It is no more a straight way, and also there is talk of an oath to him as well."

"But how has this happened, my Lord Father?" I asked.

"Listen then, my son Drogo!" he said and banged his fist on the side of the chair. "My grandfather swore his oath to the Great Charles on the battle-field in the Saxon war. To the king himself. And was given his lands to hold for the King so that he could always have strong fighting men ready if there was need. And that was good. And you, my son, we gave you your royal name out of love for the great Charles. To tie you to the King of the Franks."

"And your own father?" I asked in a soft voice.

"How was his oath?"

"He took an oath to be passed on with his name written down. But an oath to a good and loyal servant of King Louis. But now — " His face twisted and I waited for him to go on. "Now I must go to a man I cannot trust. And to whom I shall find myself bound!"

"How can this be?" I asked. "Surely he will pass on the oaths?"

"I do not trust him," my father said and he looked around as if someone might be listening. "The Count of Paris before him, Count Gerard, he left the King's service. Took himself off to Lothar. With all his riches and all his family. That was three years back and now — there is this new Count. I know little about him, but if Gerard, who came of a great family, yes, related even to the Royal house — if he went over because Lothar was the oldest son, and he's now strong in the eastern part of Frank-land, so that we hear of fighting all the time and those who are unlucky in choosing their masters get tonsured or blinded..." And here my father began muttering angrily about people and places that meant nothing to me.

At last I said, "If the oaths are put into writing they will surely go to the King." I was feeling sad inside myself that I would not see the King, but what mattered truly was the oath.

"Yet if this man comes between -" my father said.

"He cannot do that, Lord my Father," I said. "He, too, is bound."

But my father swung back. "The King gave my grandfather his lands of which I am now Lord. They were his gift, his thanks, to him as a Frank, knowing he would always do right, leading his fighting men to the King's help. For me it was the same. He led our men into Saxony. Those were good old times, fighting the Saxons. And I myself, I led our men against the Saracens. Before we Franks started fighting one another. Good days. Now I do not know which way to look."

"So you are troubled," I said softly.

"Yes," he said. "These are bad times. My father had his share of the great Charles' glory. King Louis ruled well in other ways. But he did rule. Because of his wishes I gave you to the monks to learn. Do you understand all this?"

"Yes," I said. "I do understand. But the times have changed?" And suddenly it came to me that my father was deeply unhappy and that he wanted my help. "Tell me," I said. "What do you fear?"

He gave a kind of gasp and stood up from his chair and began to walk around. "It seems that I must make my oath only through the Count of Paris and — in a way — to him. I am told that my lands are not truly mine, they belong to the Count as part of the Count's domain and I only hold them as — as — a follower of this Count who was put here in this diocese by the King but is himself only another man, as I am! I am to become his thing, his vassal, and to send or lead my men, not when I choose — as I chose myself out of love and duty to my King to lead them to stop the Saracen raids — but as this Count may demand. That is — not to be any longer a free Frank as I have always been, as you, Drogo, were to be after me!"

He looked at me in a way I had never seen him

do. I tried to think what to say. At last I asked, "And if you do not take this oath?"

"Then he could send men, a great host of men, to plunder my lands, saying they were his, that I was a rebel!"

"Surely that would be so wrong that all would see it. Totally against the Commandments. Coveted! Does this Count admit that his own power comes from God?"

"There was a Bishop and some lesser clergy when his messenger, who was, I think, his uncle, came to tell me what I must do. And brought gold to buy me. And sweet words. Making it all look good. And it seemed -" His voice broke and I could see that he was shamed. I looked away. He went on, "They said my name would go to the King. But now..." And his voice dropped.

I thought about this. I had seen these people who had come from the Count but had not known what their errand was. I had kept out of their way. When this Bishop paid his visit to my Abbot they had spoken together, but I do not think my Abbot knew that this Bishop's talk about the oath meant what it now seemed to mean. Or maybe they only spoke about spiritual things.

At last I said, "Lord my Father, if this Count tries to twist your oath to the King into an oath to himself, and I think this is in your mind, and if this Count does things which no Frank should do, if above all, he himself is not loyal to the King, then, as certain as a stone drops, your oath is no more valid."

He said, "That, I think is true, but he is very strong. He might try to take my lands, on some pretence."

It seemed, strangely, that my strong father was asking for help. I said, "I do not think that our Lord God, who is our true Lord, would allow this to happen. Our Abbot — my Abbot — would stand against it. He would go to this Bishop whom you saw, would take him into argument and surely no bad deed would be allowed. I am sure of that. Also, the new Abbot of St. Denis is a friend of our Abbot and a man full of justice and also power. Perhaps -" and I thought very carefully — "you should take this oath and if this Count shows himself to be wicked, a traitor or an oppressor, then the part of the oath which belongs to him is no more valid. You will still be your own man in the sight of God and the Franks and you will still be loyal to the King."

And then I said, "I will take all this to the Abbot and I am very sure he will give the same counsel." And I hunted in my mind for a text from Holy Writ which would say what I meant, so that any oath which my father took would depend for its validity on the worthiness — or not — of the Count.

All at once I saw my father's face change. He came over and laid a hand on my shoulder. "I will do as you say, my son," he said. "I will take the oath, knowing it becomes invalid if the Count becomes unworthy of it. I see that you are becoming a young man of sense and justice. If only, yes, if only the good King Louis had been still living, I would have taken you to him, even the long journey to Aachen, to show him another true Frank. But maybe we shall get to see young King Charles and then all will be well."

So we went on through the great lands of the

Count of Paris. Most of it looked prosperous enough. But as we rode along the river Seine, broader than any I had seen, we came on signs of something new and dreadful. Two villages had been plundered by the Danes who had come up the river Seine in their terrible war-ships, so quick and secret that people had no time to protect themselves or even to escape into the forests carrying what they could. Now there were only burnt timbers and one or two families trying to build at least some shelter, and always some who were still shattered, weeping for children or wives or for their slaughtered beasts and their plundered church.

My father riding beside me, said, "These Danes are our worst enemies now. These last few years they have been coming up out of the sea and there are as many as fish in that same sea. Worse than the Saracens."

I asked, "They are heathens, the Danes?"

"Yes," he said. "But if we could destroy their idols as those of the Saxons were destroyed, then surely we would win against them."

"Did that happen with the Saxons?" I asked.

"Yes, yes," he said, and laughed. "The great Charles tore down their idol, the Irminsul, smashed it to bits in its evil temple and took all the gold, like a dragon's gold. Then they had the choice, baptism or death. Ha! So the Saxons became Christians and obedient to the Empire."

I remember that I thought this a great thing, also I was glad to my heart that my father was speaking to me as though I was a man.

At last we came to the place which my Abbot had

told me about, knowing I would go there since it was close to the city of Paris. This was the great monastery of Saint Denis. All had been rebuilt in the time of the Great Charles who had awarded it a splendid donation. It was not only that the small church with the bodily remains of the Saint himself (and his fellows who had been beheaded by the heathen Goths) had been enlarged and made more beautiful with carvings and pillars, but there were guest halls and long cloisters between the buildings so that we need never get rained on. The food was good and the privies were clean.

The Abbot Hilduin, of whom I had heard much praise from my own Abbot, had died a few years back, but it was in a way as though he were still there, for his sayings and orders were often repeated, especially the stories of the other Denis saints who in some way were entwined with one another. It was he who had brought in the Benedictine orders and prayers and had thrown out all who were not truly living the monastic life. It was wonderful to know that there was always a group of monks at prayer, keeping the life-line between earth and heaven.

Hilduin's successor, the Abbot Louis, was in a way, almost greater, seeing that he was arch-chancellor to young King Charles, and indeed a close relative, since he was a grandson of the great Charles. Haimo laughed about this, saying that the King and the Abbot were like himself and me, since the Abbot had been born out of wedlock but they had the same grandfather. I did not mind him saying this to me, but I warned him not to let it slip.

 Once, when I was sitting quietly at my father's feet, Abbot Louis came and spoke to my father about

Count Gerard, how wickedly he had left, taking all his goods and followers over to King Lothar. Yet the new Count would be loyal to King Charles — at least so he said — but I felt that perhaps he was saying this as some kind of test, to find out my father's loyalty. They were speaking in the noble tongue and my father sometimes stumbled over words or mis-heard something. But I was able to give a little help and the Abbot praised my Latin.

There was so much for me to turn over in my mind, up in the room which had been given to Haimo and me. Here we must wait until the Count was ready to receive us. It was a pleasant room. The floor was dry earth, but it was well trodden-in and there was enough hay and blankets for our comfort. They fed us well and I went often into the church to see and admire all there was in it.

Haimo was supposed to be my servant, but neither he nor I thought of it that way. He could read and he knew his Scripture, though sometimes he laughed at things which I had always thought very serious.

His uncle had taught us both how to shoot with a hunting bow and also how to use spear and sword. He had brought with him two boy-sized mail coats, "because," he said, "you never know." We had plenty of games together and I could see how many a fine tale or fine doing might be turned upside down and this could be our joke, even sometimes when reading the Scriptures. Haimo cared well for the horses and he saw to the washing of my linen which needed it by now.

Once he came in and said he had spoken to a girl, one of the maids who brought in our beer, and he thought she would play with us. But I said, No, no, remembering what my Abbot had said about temptation.

We were getting impatient to move on. Several times my father sent for me. I even dared once to correct his Latin and he only laughed. Now and then he would speak about the oath, going over his anxieties.

"But let us wait, my Lord Father," I said. "God will surely guide us." And he seemed easier. All this was deep happiness to me.

Haimo saw what had happened between my father and I and would have teased me a little, but I would not have it and spoke coldly to him. Yet I was sorry when I saw he was hurt. It is difficult to find oneself being two different persons; inside myself I was still Haimo's friend and half-brother, but I had also become my father's trusted friend — something I had never thought possible.

AS WE RODE

on along the banks of the river, we met another party, a small Lord, his wife and some followers. He and my father had much talk, mostly about fighting they had both been in, (though not near one another) and about mistakes which had been made by the com- manders. I did not speak much, but I listened, glad that my father felt him- self steadier. He was finding out all this time about the Count — what kind of man he was and how much or how little he followed in the ways that the Great Charles had brought to be the pattern for us Franks.

And so at last we came to the place where the

river divides, making the island which is Paris and no easy place for an attack, since there are stone and timber fortifications all round it, guarded night and day. There are many bridges, including one great one with huge stones going down into the water in a way I had never seen before. There were little houses along the bridge and gates at each end. These were barred and heavy, but we were let through and a party with brightly coloured clothes and small banners came to meet and welcome us. They had good horses, corn-fed and lively.

When we got to our lodgings I asked them to give us corn for my Suelde and Haimo's little horse as well as for my father's great horse, and plenty of hay and straw for the rest. I would not have dared to ask a short time back, but now I felt I was almost a man. I could speak strongly, though always courteously. Later, when we were speaking with greater people, it seemed to me that their Latin was at least no better than mine and some important words were not said right. Not, at least, as my Abbot would have spoken them.

Still, we were well housed. Our men were given a high-pitched room with a good fire, as much meat, porridge and beer as they wanted brought in by cheerful, easy girls. I wondered if they had thought about the meaning of the oath my father was to take. The special guests went up steps, and streaks of sunlight appeared on the wooden floors when we opened the shutters and looked down on the busy town.

My father had a great bed with carved wood at the head. There was a cheerful, fattish woman, decently dressed, who was there to help him with everything he wanted. From the laughing and squeaking we heard it was just that. Walakind could, I think, have had the same if he had wanted it.

Haimo and I had a room together with straw beds, washed sheep skins over the straw. I took out of my pack the fine cloak with gold trimmings which were spoil from the battle of Barcelona, a long while back; it had been well washed and was fit for any court. I had also light shoes of Spanish leather and the new hose my mother had given me before we left, along with three white linen shirts, so I was well equipped. I had a small, silver-hilted dagger which my father had worn as a boy, but my best things were my great belt buckle, bronze and silver, and the brooch which I have had since my baptism. It has a thin gold edge and inside it tiny enclosures like very far-off fields which, seen together, make the picture of Saint Perpetua, my patron saint: I knew all her story — how she and her friends, some of them her servants, went cheerful and singing to be martyred in the arena by wild beasts. My mother had told it to me first, but then my teachers had told me more. In a sense I was in her care, but she also in mine. I promised to fight to the death anyone who insulted her, but that never happened. Instead I was often asked to tell people all about her.

There are many saints in Paris. Perhaps St. Genevieve has the most followers and the most beautiful church with the best furnished altar. But there is also St. Germain with his great Abbey, while everywhere there are stories and sometimes paintings of noble Abbots and Bishops, such as Bishop Landry, the friend of St. Eloi, who gave away all his church silver and gold to feed his congregation in the year when harvests failed.

I duly went to Confession, mostly, I think, because of the great beauty of the churches and the pleasant smell, after the streets, where it was hard to get away from the stink of crowded people and kitchen smoke or sometimes rotting fish. Through my small penances I felt myself to be back in the Abbey among my teachers, and not unhappy and anxious, at least not about the present difficult things.

Most of the churches and Abbeys had been built recently, but others perhaps in a grandfather's grandfather's time. Yet there were ruins that went back further to the days of the heathen Romans, who held the greatest Empire in the world: in the time of the Emperor Constantine that Empire began to turn into our own Empire, though not without pain. There remained the walls of their palaces, baths, monuments, and part of a circus where perhaps martyrs had suffered. It is said that King Pippin had lived in one of the palaces. But Paris was full of stories and if you listened too much you could get entangled in thinking about the dead, which is good if they are saints or martyrs, but less good if they are small kings.

It seems that the Romans built drains to take away all foul matters, but this is not our custom in Frank-land, though perhaps it might be in a royal palace. Here in Paris, at the down end of the island there was a great gate where the carriers of night soil and refuse from shops and tanneries and such could dump their loads into the river. So the city was kept clean, though it can never smell like meadow or forest. Nor is there much room for garden and orchard except in the case of a few great houses.

Haimo and I, not wearing the clothes of the city, and looking about and perhaps pointing and laughing, would be accosted by people, among them women. We became quick at escaping, though once or twice, we met with some who were truly friendly and God-loving. By asking questions we found out that there were two other Lords here with their men, who had come to take the Oath.

There was much coming and going around our place and we were well fed. There was wine, which I like less than our own beer, and also there were new kinds of cakes, some very delicious. My father had me sit by him at the top table. Besides the good food we had small glass bowls to wash our fingers after meat. I had never seen this custom, but it was pleasant. The little bowls were pale blue, like flowers. For drinking, too, we had glass at our table. I thought it made the wine look better, but my father did not care for them. He liked to bang his wine or beer down on the table and you cannot do that with glass.

Walakind and Haimo were at a lower table where there was more talk and joking and young people, and the food was as good, or almost. They picked up the jokes and gossip that go about and sometimes tell more than courteous speech. It was not all good. Some of the smaller clergy sat at that table and seemed to be as merry as the rest, telling bawdy stories, which angered Walakind a little.

As for me, I had a sad time with an oldish woman, an aunt of the Count wearing many rings and jewels hung around her neck, some pretty enough; but she wanted to pull me close to her and stroke my neck and what other parts of me she could lay hands on.

My father laughed but I did not like it.

But there were other women. When I went, remembering my best manners, to pay my duties to the wife and daughters of the Count, they gave me many sweetmeats, and indeed sweet kisses. They had a garden with sunny walls, up which grew fruit trees and flowers all new to me. I had never seen roses so beautiful, and there was a great vine. I must needs dance a round with the young girls, and the eldest kissed me on the cheek in courteous fashion, so I wondered whether perhaps the Count of Paris was not as bad as my father had feared.

The Count had many beautiful things and strange, more than our own Abbey had. There was, for one thing, a golden bowl with figures on it, winged horses and little people with swords and shields, wearing only short cloaks so that one must laugh at them. But they were as clear as life, and so were the horses and cattle on another golden plate. I think they were made long, long ago by the people who lived in the world before us Franks or the old Romans, and had no chance of salvation. So where were their souls I wondered?

And how had all these things come to the Count? I heard stories or parts of stories, and it seemed that justice had been twisted, the justice which the great Charles had left for those he had honoured to carry on. Rewards had been given to the Count for doings which should have been shameful. Haimo had overhead talk and brought it to me, but what could I do? My father did not want to listen.

There was often talk about the late Count Gerard. I listened to both sides, carefully not giving any opinion. Many thought he had done well by shifting his allegiance from our King Charles to old King Lothar. In a way it was a family matter. The sister of the Count's wife was married to Lothar; that would have meant something, surely.

He had of course taken his following with him, all his moveable goods, his horses and hounds, servants and slaves. But the hole in the wall was quickly patched up. The Bishops who had not, except for (and then there was much laughing and naming which I did not entirely understand or like) been on the side of Lothar, saw to the new appointment. They had chosen a Count who would suit them and the young King who was already showing himself a winner.

I found all this hard to come to grips with, above all the laughter at what was surely of deep import. How did it affect the oaths of loyalty? Had they changed with the name of the King? What had the oath-takers said or done about it? It seemed, nothing. I tried to talk to my father about this, but it was truly something he did not care even to think about. He gave me money to buy small things and indeed there is plenty to buy in Paris from all over the world, though most of it needs hard bargaining.

There was talk about other great Lords, Counts, Margraves, Dukes, which of them were well and which ill disposed to the Count of Paris; how many armed men they had, which had gone to King Lothar when Count Gerard left, and — there would be laughter here — whom they were related to; above all who could be called upon to fight off the Danes or send parties around to take them in the rear if they came up the Seine.

Yet nothing was spoken about the Empire, the

fears and anxieties about the movements of the wicked Empire of Byzantium, and the Saracens across the Eastern mountains who might suddenly move. Nor were the great hopes talked about that we Franks have held and surely will always hold, for they brought us together: the strength of heart under God which should be uniting us Franks and its burden of care and responsibility for all Christendom. I could feel it in me. I could hear the voice of my Abbot. But I could not speak of it and also I knew that if I had spoken it could have made matters worse for my father.

When I went over the day's talk I was sad. It seemed to me that these people, whatever their rank, were destroying something which had been built up over the generations. It had been lived for and died for and had great beauty. It was all because they only cared about power, and this power was built on riches of one kind or another. That was how marriages were arranged, how land was swapped about, so that poor, honest people might suddenly find themselves with a new lord whom they did not care for. Was this doing God's will?

Yes, there was a Lord Bishop, whose ring I kissed, kneeling, but he seemed no more far-sighted than the rest. He too thought only of the diocese of Paris and how its riches could be increased, and about the gold that was needed to frame the altar in the new church which he was building. He did not even once call on the loyalty and courage of those around him, my fellow Franks, to defend the Empire of Rome and Christendom which the great Charles left to us. I felt myself getting hot and angry, wishing I could in some way turn the talk round. And the day was now

46

fixed when my father was to take the great oath, and I with him.

I could let down my guard with Haimo and speak my mind. He too had been well treated, also had more freedom, could find new friends and listen to the gossip, which he could then pass to me. One day when I came back, a little angry from the great hall of the Count, I found Haimo talking with a tall, tow-haired lad, a bit older than myself, wearing a coat of good leather, and a lump of amber hanging from a thong, but no dagger at his belt. "This is Wolfin," said Haimo. "He is a Saxon, a real one, but tame. You can push him over!"

I was angry with Haimo for not preparing me. Was this a free man? What should I do? Then the Saxon put out his hand and I felt bound to take it. "That's right," said Haimo. "He doesn't bite. His Gods are dead as stockfish. Stinking!"

The young man scowled and then I saw that Haimo was saying this just to make me take the other side. "No need to use bad words," I said, and took the lad's hand firmly.

At that he said quickly, "I am held as a hostage. My life is not my own. But while I live can we be friends?"

"God be with you," I said. "It is hard to be a hostage. Hard, too, for your father and mother."

"My father is dead," said the lad and repeated, "Dead. Dead! My mother — she has gone to my father. It is my uncles for whom I am in bond. They could yet become strong and a danger to — you."

"Well," I said, "this is bad talk for a first meeting, Wolfin," for I had remembered his name. "Come, let

47

us look at the horses."

Out of the corner of my eye I saw Haimo grinning. He had in some way intended this to happen. I went to the boy and put my arm through his and I thought that some day I would ask him about the amber. Meantime it was strange to have taken the hand of a Saxon and I wondered what was in his mind about me.

BEFORE I go on to tell what happened and how it went after the oath-taking, I must tell about the Saxon, Wolfin.

In that place, Paris, he was part of my life and part of Haimo's. He was closer to us than any in the court of the Count. During all those summer months, we three were much together. I knew that if only I could save him for Christendom, it would be the best deed of my life.

Here, then, is the story of Wolfin, that came out bit by bit, mostly from his talking to me, or when suddenly struck by bitter anger, perhaps tears; but I have filled it in from what I heard when I listened to the talk of older people. It is also what I was told by one of the monks at St. Genevieve's who had been in a monastery attacked by a band of Saxon outlaws; wolves, he said, wolves, that would roast in hell forever. Yet perhaps most of this story comes from Haimo. I think that Haimo is kinder than I am, but that is also because he is less strict than I try to be, so that Wolfin found it easier to talk to him. Indeed it all started when Wolfin had been punished by one of the Count's servants for some rudeness he had been charged with, and Haimo came on him in his misery, and gentled or teased him out of it. It is a long story, going back beyond our time.

It is very many years ago that the Irminsul, the great hideous Pagan thing, was pulled down and broken into bits and the huge treasures piled in the temple were taken by the army of the Great Charles. After that most of the Saxons gave themselves up and were baptised in great groups but always with holy water. They then became part of the Empire of Christendom, not Franks, but like their younger brothers.

Only, some of them never accepted baptism. They went away into wild places. They made images and worshipped them, so they are doubtless in hell. Sometimes they were hunted and if it was found that they were still worshipping these images, they were treated in the same way that idolators were treated in the Old Testament. Or indeed as the great Romans did with Carthage. That is, they were wiped out.

Yet must we always do this? Are we certain that, in spite of all our sins, we are so much better than they are? I ask my Abbot and he says that we are God's children, accepted through baptism. We must do God's will as a good child does the will of his

Father, and it must be God's will to wipe out all worship of other gods or idols. Sometimes I am so sure that I am a child of God. But then again, not.

So the heathen Saxons were killed like vermin. Sometimes a woman would be spared and kept as a concubine, but of course baptised. Was that better or worse? Women, poor creatures, cannot be totally responsible for their own souls. I think of my aunt who is an Abbess and is certainly learned, for she is now writing a book of morals, which I have heard much praised by those who have seen it. Nonetheless, when she comes to our house and table, she is for ever asking help or advice about one thing or another.

Well then, there were a few families who had, it seems, been nobles among the Saxons and had not taken part in the great surrender to the mercy of the Emperor Charles and the enormous baptism that followed. Some were hunted out, over the years, and destroyed, since they had become like rats nibbling at the edges of the Empire of Christendom. But there was a pack of them in the wild country to the east, beyond what is now, unhappily I think, the kingdom of Lothar, but was then under the rule of the Emperor Louis, son of the great Charles. And here Wolfin was born and brought up as a pagan, hating Christendom because it had killed so many of his people and was totally the enemy. I can almost see how it must have been for them, although I do not like to think of it.

His father taught him to fight when he was only a young boy. He was, I think, the eldest of three or four children and so closest to his father perhaps. He spoke to me (not at once but after he had come to trust me a little) about his father, who, in his mind, was brave and generous and loving: an image of what he himself wanted to become. They were all, of course, pagans. I do not know and I do not wish to know what devils they worshipped, nor would he have told me that. But I believe he took some kind of oaths or went through some kind of ceremony. It was all past, long past, yet it came into his dreams. I hate to think of it. Indeed I stopped him even speaking of it.

But he had been happy. He loved his home, poor though it was, for his family had lost most of their goods during the years of war. His grandfather had been killed. So Wolfin had grown up, knowing that they had lost to their enemies, but had kept their pride. Yet, as we know, pride is of the evil one and always must fall to the power of the angels, which is penitence and admission of sin.

Besides his father there were uncles and others of his kin, some well armed. They were like a thorn in the side of the Empire. It was said that they had murderously attacked certain good farms in the valley, which belonged to Christians, tenants of a monastery on the borders of safe Frankish land. This may well be true, but whether or no, there was fighting when an armed force was sent in to keep order and protect the monastery lands. Wolfin's father was killed and, he believed, his mother, since he never heard of her again.

He himself had fought at his father's side, but had been knocked over by a horse and tied up before he could get to his feet. He saw his father dead, an arrow through his throat. Their house was burned and I hate to think on what he told me happened to his young sisters. Such things should not be.

Wolfin, wounded, was taken to the monastery where his wounds were dressed, and he was also baptised. He had not agreed nor had they asked for his agreement. It happened and made his hate of the Franks and their belief — our belief — stronger, worse. I tried to tell him that this had been meant solely for his good, but the hate was still too hot to let him listen. It seems that a little brother was also baptised, but then taken away. Wolfin never heard of him again. Ever.

He was told that he was being held as hostage for his uncles and other kin. If they broke the peace of the Empire again, he would die. They had been told this, so there could be no revenge for his father and his family. Now he must learn to speak — even to dream — in Frankish. He must learn to say prayers by rote. He was held at first in some camp in the eastern lands, but then handed over to the Count of Paris, that is the Count Gerard; Franks were all the same to him. He was exchanged like a piece of meat. Our Wolfin. Why do we like one person more than another? Surely God has some part in this!

I had a little money from my father and we bought small things and ate fried bits, or smoked river fish from the corner stalls. I remember I bought a little copper bell for my brother Malfrid but, even as I thought of him playing with it and laughing, he was already dead of that quick stomach pain which had seized him, and, as I hope and trust, was taken into heaven. Also I bought, at the Church of St. Geneviève, a little painting on vellum, of the Blessed Virgin; that was for my sister. I am sure she has it still.

From time to time I would lead Wolfin, as if by chance, into a church. I would take his hand and tell him, as though it were only a story, about the saints and the angels, the constant coming and going between earth and heaven, between ourselves and God. He would pull away from me sometimes and not listen, but he was afraid to be out of touch, and besides, as I came to understand him, he truly liked me. For my part I was beginning to feel I had a kind of duty to him.

Yet it was difficult. He could not see any beauty in a church and he would pull away if I knelt beside an altar. However it was so beautiful with the candles lighting up the darkness, the soft puff of incense, the movements and singing of the choir, different from one church to another, the colour and richness of the robes worn to God's glory. I could not but be happy and I wanted the three of us, Wolfin, Haimo and myself, to be happy together.

Sometimes, in the street afterwards, he would make fun of angels, which I found sad and hurtful, yet I pretended to laugh with him and then explained that the angels were a symbol for heaven and lightness. I told him about heaven and what good people could expect after their death, but if he listened even a little I knew it was out of friendship, not out of any kind of belief.

Perhaps if I had found easy friendship among the Count's followers or family, I would have spent less time with Wolfin. But that had not happened. Certainly there were many I spoke with and more, perhaps, that Haimo spoke with, though I felt that some of these were on another level and I must be cautious with them. Some I was a little friendly with from time to time and joined in their games and sports. I liked the hunting, when we crossed the river in flat barges holding our horses' bridles. Also there were wild strawberries in the fields over there, bigger and sweeter than our own at home.

There was one boar hunt when I did well, and, I am afraid, boasted of it. At least my father was pleased, and so was Walakind. He, I knew, was jealous of my liking for the Abbey and afraid I might decide to join that great community. He should have understood that, although I loved that life of the mind and soul, I knew that my first duty must be to take my father's place when the time came and, as far as in me lay, to practice justice and mercy on those who would then be mine.

But often I felt sad talking with a fellow hunter or player, for these followers of the Count, as I must think of them, spoke about Kings and Bishops in a way that seemed to go against all my own hopes, loyalties and the strong patterns I had set for myself. Some had sworn to Count Gerard, yet had not gone with him to King Lothar, and the reasons seemed to have nothing to do with the oaths they had taken, but only of where their own interests lay. So I always felt uneasy when I was with them.

Also it seemed that the present Count of Paris, although he professed great loyalty to young King Charles, might easily slip across if the reward was to be greater. I got the feeling that there might well be plots and promises and perhaps a killing or two, and all between Franks. There was laughing about all this, but I did not like it. No! I felt sick to my soul sometimes and I knew my father too had this feeling, it seemed more and more that this oath we would be

55

called to take might bind us into a kind of evil. In my grandfather's day it could never have been like this. Nor perhaps even in the days of King Louis. But now?..

For me, it meant that I would walk off and find Haimo and often Wolfin with him. We played children's games with sticks and pebbles or we wandered about Paris where there were so many people that two or three more are not noticed. We watched men at work on metal — and it might be anything from copper to gold — or wood or leather. We watched the weaving of fine cloth, the building of boats or carts, the making of chain mail and the blowing of glass. I had seen some crafts at the Abbey, especially writing and painting, but much in the city of Paris was new to me and certainly to Haimo and Wolfin.

CHAPTER FIVE ─────────────────────────────

SO CAME the day of the oath-taking. The day before I had
asked my father's leave to ride out to the great
church of St. Denis, where I would be among the
Benedictines. I
wanted to be as
pure as mortal
man could be and
that was how I
felt when, after
deep prayer, I
came back. I had
not eaten and had
strange dreams
that night; it see-
med that in them
I had fought and
overcome the
devils that had
sometimes fright-
ened me so much.
Now they were
gone, along with my childhood which was now
totally behind me. It must be as a man that I faced

the oath-taking.

I fastened my father's cloak with the great brooch in which I could see, as though far off, Christ on the cross. The stuff of the cloak had a pattern woven into it, and gold along the edges; it had been his grandfather's gift from the great Charles. Once, when I was a child and ill with a fever, my mother had laid it across me and soon I was well and the fever gone. Again, there were my father's best riding boots which he was to wear now; when I was a child I loved to run my finger along the stags' heads embossed on the leather.

I said quietly, "Remember, Lord my Father, that the oath goes two ways. If the catch slips you are no more bound." I wanted him to understand, deep down, that if the Count showed himself unworthy, if the passing on of the oath to the King meant nothing, then the oath dropped. And I knew that something wrong was on the way unless we could stop it from coming into our lives as free Franks. We would find ourselves tied to great lords and forced into obedience over actions which we knew were wrong, and it might happen that we would begin to treat our own men in the same way, tying them to our services, although they, like ourselves, were free Franks, new Roman citizens, guardians of Christendom.

I myself was well clad and had washed with soap. I followed my father into the great hall of the Count, keeping my eyes down but yet seeing looks here and there. There were Haimo and Walakind and the men who had come with us — but how few they looked in the great press of the Count's subjects and courtiers! Haimo managed to glance around through fingers not quite closed over his face. He told me afterwards of looks, most of all from two bishops — for there was another come for the ceremony — and the lesser clergy. The paintings and hangings on the walls showed scenes from the Gospels, but for me there was no feeling of God's presence.

When our names and the names of our lands were called, we were escorted to the Count, who sat, a gold circlet on his head and wearing a great cloth of scarlet with gold woven into it, in the centre of a vast bench covered with splendid, many-coloured cloth, the Bishop beside him. There were other clergy, in full robes, at each side, as well as a tall monk who wrote down our names and the title to our lands, in order I suppose, to send to the King's Chancery. We had to kneel, but on cushions, so that the kneeling was not that of a servant. My father spoke first; then I did. Next we rose and were embraced by the Count, which I did not care for. Nor, I think, did my father, least of all since the Count kissed me on the mouth.

It was the same for the other two Lords. Both of them had sons and daughters, but none were old enough to take the oath which I had taken. It was a pity, as I would have liked to find out how it seemed to them; I could not ask the two Lords. After the oath-taking there was a banquet and, because I had not eaten for a day, I ate too much and was sick in the night, which showed that I should have kept my fast for longer, two days at least. Perhaps I would have done that if the oath had been to the anointed King himself.

I had watched the two other Lords taking their oaths, and I could see the same anxiety in their faces, the same questioning about all they might be exchanging — for what? Later, speaking with some of their folk, I got to know that they had tried ways of not coming. Both came, as we did, from the further parts of the Count's lands — or rather of his Bishop's diocese, for all was done in the name of this great 'diocese of Paris', which had spread itself over the years, so that Count and Bishop became a double power. It seemed that the same unwelcome message had been sent out to most of the lesser Lords such as my father, and had been similarly talked over and if possible delayed. All had felt that this was the beginning of something dire, that the Counts were becoming too much like Kings. Yet, on the face of it, we had only given our due and proper oath to our King. It was the feeling behind it that was wrong.

Also it appeared that there was someone who had been summoned and had not arrived; so what would happen now? Could we be called upon to fetch this man by force — putting ourselves and our own fighting men into jeopardy — not against Avars or Saracens or Danes, but against our own blood? I begged my father to go home soon, before we became taken up in this evil situation. He said he would if he could, but having just taken the oath it would look bad if he neglected it so soon.

"They will send messengers, they will threaten," he said, " and so perhaps this man after all will come. Perhaps it will be forgotten."

But I could see that he did not truly think so. Sometimes we would ride out of Paris for a hunt. I tried my hand at fishing in the river Seine, but got little. All the time I was anxious.

So what could we do? My father felt a deep

60

sadness. If he had taken this oath to the anointed King, there would have been a true binding, even perhaps a kind of happiness, a passion. It would have been as true for both. But not here. Haimo and I watched him. He was drinking heavily and the Count's wine was stronger than ours ever was. I could understand that, but he did not choose to talk with me again and that made me sad. And to one of the women, (not the fat one, but better dressed, able to play the small harp and sing) he gave a jewel which I remembered he had promised to my sister. I wished we could go home. I wished I could talk again with my Abbot for there was so much that I needed to understand and it was not only my father and his troubles. I had been talking so much with Wolfin, the Saxon hostage, that indeed we three were sometimes laughed at for going so often together, Haimo, Wolfin and I. Because I had said I was his friend in a way that he had taken as meaningful (and indeed it was meant so), Wolfin spoke openly of how he hated the Count of Paris and all his followers.

When he spoke of his father as he sometimes did — for it seemed to burst out of him and here and there he used a word that I could not understand, so it must have been from Saxon speech — it was clearly of someone he had loved dearly. Yet Wolfin's father was a man who had murdered and raided, attacking the small monasteries which preached and converted in the lands that had lately come in to the Empire. I knew that his band of Saxons were wolves, hell-bound. They had to be wiped out, or at least stopped by any kind of force from doing more harm. It was likely enough that his uncles had been tamed and were no longer a danger but Wolfin would still be kept — in case.

I also think that, even as a young boy, Wolfin had taken certain vows, but I stopped him when I felt he was near to telling me, since they were heathen vows and I would have to be angry with him. When he spoke bitterly of his baptism, I wondered but could not ask whether this holy water stung him, for I heard it had done so to Saracens baptised as part of our conquest. All this was painful. Meanwhile he was being punished for the sins of others, and I felt that God would want me to lift some of the punishment off him. And perhaps, someday I might succeed in this...

Meanwhile his pain went on. It is always bad to be a hostage, but he had been teased, hit, poked with daggers, laughed at and threatened; worst by a younger son of the Count of Paris, a spoiled brat who also liked whipping his father's dogs. It was getting more then he could bear, but what could he do?

There came a day when Wolfin suddenly started to cry in a way I hated to see a strong boy cry. It was when he was telling us how we Franks had pulled down and broken the Saxons' pagan image, their idol, the Irminsul. Of course this was right and proper, undeniably, because this idol of theirs was keeping them from God, so that in fact we Franks were giving them the greatest gift in the world, could they but understand this. But it was not so for them, although at first it was hard for me to twist it round in my mind. I saw my friend hurt to the bottom of his heart because it was the sign of his people, it was their loyalty, it meant to them something more important than God's love and truth. I tried to comfort him, saying that when that thing was broken, the way became open for them to attain heaven and life everlasting beyond our understanding. Some of his people saw this and took the right way, willingly.

"My people did not want that," said Wolfin. "Your heaven is our prison."

I tried to put my mind close to his. "Surely you wish to be saved from hell-fire, from an eternity of torture? That was why we took and baptised all the crowds of you Saxons. To save you for God. Your leaders asked for baptism."

"It was that or death," said Wolfin. "My uncles accepted and are dishonoured. But we did not accept, my father and I. Although they did this thing to me afterwards. My father went to our Gods. I want to go where he is. I deny this baptism. I hate your God!"

I did not know what to say. It was a terrible thing to hear. I could not have repeated what he said. Only I knew that he was dreadfully unhappy, wounded in his deepest loyalty. Later I might try to argue with him, show him the truth, indeed I knew I would have to do this, but now I must try to comfort him with the ample store of the true compassion which, as a Christian, I could draw out from the eternal sources.

I put my arm round him and started to talk about other things which might soften his hurt and anger. We had light bows to shoot at marks or sometimes at birds. He had not been allowed even a knife for cutting bread at table and was clumsy when I lent him my bow, so I gave a look to Haimo who was a good bowman but now shot wild on purpose, cursing himself and jumping about, in a way giving pleasure to Wolfin and building him up a little so that he managed at last a good shot for it. It was clear that he was able with a bow, but it had been taken from him, like everything else but the amber. I think he had said this amber would kill anyone else, but one day he let me hold it. I felt that this was perhaps a little step. If he could trust me over this, which was yet a piece of his deepest self, he might in the end trust me to lead him into salvation. I talked often about the joys of heaven and how we would be together, free and equal, un-hurt and un-hurting, for ever and ever. I told him about the saints and the martyrs who had walked into death knowing of the safety beyond the grave. I cannot know how much he listened or whether he only listened because it was the voice of a friend. Haimo did not join in so much with this.

As for myself, I would need to ask my Abbot what was the hope for one who was formally baptised, by force and without agreement for it seemed that if he could swallow the great draughts of compassion which I hoped to give him, then he might see the light. I knew I could neither force nor bribe him. I began also to turn over in my mind how I would ask my father to have the Saxon transferred into his care. Surely that would not be too difficult. Once away from Paris and all he hated, Wolfin would take in all I had to say. Oh it was a good dream.

My father from time to time was troubled about this friendship of mine, but he was too much troubled about other things to give it much attention. One of the other oath-takers, a Lord called Flodard, who had lands somewhere south of the Isle of Paris, was as concerned as my father about forcing the fourth of the noble Franks who had been called for the oath-taking but had refused to come. "We have enemies enough to keep our swords bright," he said. "This would rust them."

My father had told Walakind that he and two other of our men were to ride back and raise another band of good men who would threaten and if need be use force on the one who would not take the oath and who, it was said, was building strong walls and getting men and horses and food in behind them. Walakind did not at all want to do this and argued with my father, as one Frank to another, but in the end he was my father's man. He grumbled, but accepted that it was necessary for all our sakes.

It was now nearing the end of summer, and no news from home. Yet why should there be? I felt for Walakind. It seemed wrong that he must do this: in my mind the real enemy, the one I hated, was the Count himself. It also seemed that we had put ourselves totally in his power. Do what he says, or you lose your land, perhaps your life! The land that was given as a reward for service to our King, to the Protector of the Empire of Christendom. Given freely by the Great Charles...

IT HAD taken arguing and threatening from my father before Walakind agreed to go back with two of the others to raise the troops of our men to help in what we could only think of as a wrong action against a fellow Frank.

Meanwhile there something else was planned which I did not care for. This was to marry me to one of the Count's younger daughters. I was altogether against the idea of taking a wife, and the one they had intended for me was little more than a child. I did not even want to stroke her hair. Haimo made rough jokes about this, until I told him to stop, making my tone of voice tell him that, although he was my half-brother, he was not my equal. I had once heard my Abbot speak in this way to a monk and it had hurt me, as it did when I heard myself speak so to Haimo. But I had to do it.

I tried to have more talk with Wolfin. He was in a strange state because, although he never said so, he must have been glad to see us Franks who had been his enemies, now about to go to war with each other. One day, though, after I had come from my father who was for once in a good mood, Wolfin let drop a little more about his own father, whom he had loved so dearly. He wanted only to be like him, to be as brave, as generous, as skilled a fighter, and later as kind a father as he had been to his own young son. Ah, if we could all live like the saints, loving all men but attached to none, only to the Almighty and his Son. But which of us can cast off his affections and friendships, or rather drown them in the deep waters of love for its own sake?

So the days went by. I had never in my life tasted such good pears and plums as those in the Count's garden. There were grapes too, not our common wine grapes, but sweeter, tended in the way the old Romans had done, and many kinds of herbs and sweet roots.

My father put it to me that I might at least be betrothed to the young Princess, the Count's daughter. He tied it up with words, but Haimo said, "That means you can be in bed with her and if it goes further, that is not a great sin." Then, seeing me frowning, "But if nothing has happened and you want to marry another woman, that is no great sin either. So why not?"

But I said, "I am not interested in this matter of

sin, Haimo. But I do not want in any way to tie myself to the Count."

"Ah!" said Haimo. "That is another thing altogether and I think you are right." He added, "And so think all your father's men."

So no more was said and I was glad. Perhaps the girl was glad too, and could go on playing with other children and their dolls and toys. One marriage happened between a niece of the Count and the nephew of one of the other Lords who had taken the oath at the same time as my father. But they were both older and spent much time dancing and riding out to hunt together. For there were deer grazing along the wooded banks of the river upstream from the island of Paris, and no wild boars or bears or other forest dangers.

Sometimes, during the days we were waiting for Walakind to return, I would have one of my devil dreams in which I tried to fight with something terribly powerful and woke gasping and twisted. Yet my father now said that perhaps nothing would come of all this after all and the Lord who would not take the oath might still be persuaded or bribed.

In fact I now realized that the messengers who had come to tell my father he must take the oath, had also brought not only promises of help should we have need of it, but gold cups and silver-hilted knives. I had seen them but it had not come into my mind that they were bribes, while I think my father was sorry afterwards that he had accepted them; but perhaps if he had not, worse might have happened.

Well, he could use them now for gifts or threats. Silver and gold are, I now think, not God's, but the Great Enemy's gift to mankind. They can, surely, be used for good, but mostly they are used for evil.

By now it was the end of summer. There was one thing that was sometimes spoken about: no more raids from the Danes coming up the river. Perhaps they had destroyed so many villages and churches that they were full like wolves after a kill. I so much wished we could leave and be home again.

But then came Walakind with a new company of our men. He had sad news for me. My little brother Malfrid, the one I had most pleasure with, had died. I do not think he was poisoned or ill-wished, (for who would do such a thing among our people?) but he became sick and in spite of purging and prayer, his spirit left him. I had thought he would come running to find me and I would catch his hands and whirl him round. But no. Children are so soft. They die easily. Surely I shall see Malfrid again in heaven. But it was sad he was allowed so scant a time on earth to play.

Yet I had little time to mourn for him and as for my father, he was too anxious to be truly sad. Other fighting men had come in from the other two oath-takers, and a strong warning sent to the one who would not obey the summons. Three more days of waiting and then we would march in arms against the rebel.

I did not want to do this, nor, underneath, did my father. He too only wanted to go home, but his oath bound him and so far the Count had done us, at least, no harm. I was excited at the thought of a fight, but anxious about Suelde. A horse can be killed as easily as a man, and although Haimo and I had trained both our horses as well as we could, we could not be sure of them. We hoped the older, bigger horses could show ours what to do.

My father talked long enough with Walakind, telling him that the young ones, myself and Haimo and another two of our own age who had come with the new men, might get carried away by the feel of battle and rush into danger. He was to keep an eye on us. This was not a good war to get killed in.

Yet practice was important. We knew the killing strokes. Now was the time to try them out. I had hoped they would let Wolfin fight, arming him again so that he could feel himself a man and would be able perhaps to kill one of the Franks who were his enemies. But this was not allowed. If ever it turns out that I must have charge of a hostage, I will look on him as a brother or a son, God helping me. He will not end in hatred.

So now we were all gathered, having crossed from the city to the bank of the river, with fisher-folk all round us. Then began the trumpets and the angry songs. Haimo and I had heavy leather coats and over them the light mail shirts which had been brought with us, we wore also iron hats which we padded with leaves and moss. The horses had pieces of mail, but not enough to save them from a cut in the legs. I hoped they would be left in safety — and so it turned out. The Count's wife rode to the front, splendidly dressed and embraced her husband. There were also the daughters, including the little princess with some flowers, which she had to give me. She had been given words to say to me by her old nurse, who was half a witch, and I saw whispered in her ear, but she shook her head and she did not say them. I was a little sorry for her.

Then at last we were on the move and I kept

wondering how it would be and whether I would have to try and kill another Frank. But I was spared that. A horseman came galloping up and shouting, his horse in a cloud of sweat, his breathless and shaking. There were Danish warships sighted, coming up the river. Then, in moments, the leaders were getting together. Most of them, I think, were truly glad that everything was changed and we could now fight our real enemy. I saw this was so for my father and old Walakind, who were now shouting to our own men like boys at a game, who all beat on their shields and shouted back. I know I did myself. For now we were truly God's people, we Franks against the heathen Danes.

We all knew how the enemy came in their terrible, black, narrow, weapon-packed ships, hungry for blood and gold and women, shrieking to their heathen Gods, promising fire and death. We knew they hoped to destroy Christendom, to tear down churches and Abbeys. We knew that we Franks had been specially called to defend our Christian Empire against them, So when the Count of Paris turned the men he had gathered for one purpose into another and better one, we were all behind him, praising him as God's man, ready to die in his service.

Then I thought of something. I said to my father, "These Danes are as much the enemy of the Saxons as of ourselves. Let Wolfin the hostage fight beside us" and I added, "I am his surety. I know him. Do this for me, my father."

So it was that I raced back and found Wolfin alone and unhappy, but when I told him my father would arm him to fight the Danes, he became deeply glad and his face seemed to change. We rushed together to the gathering place and he was well welcomed and armed with sword and axe, and he thanked me from his heart. There was no spare mail, but he had a good shield with a new strap. I remember, we hugged one another.

CHAPTER SEVEN

DURING fighting, there is no time to think. Afterwards we may blame ourselves or our leaders.

This battle with the Danes was to save a small town thought to be far enough from the river to be thought safe. It was not. By the time we got there the Danes had fallen on houses, shops, beasts, burning, knifing, smashing, catching screaming women, throwing babies down wells, doing every hellish thing that Satan told them. They seemed not human and so we treated them, cutting them to pieces, throwing their 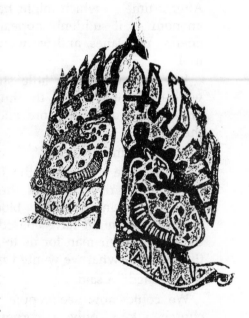 wounded back into the flames. War is the dance of sin. In this first battle I let go of the self I had built up and found another and worse self inside it. But also a self that was stronger and did not care if it hurt, or was itself hurt.

Some of the villagers and peasants had taken refuge in the church, which was stone built, but thatched, and already the Danes were throwing burning straw up onto it. We had to save that first. My father and a few of the rest, who had great horses armed with spikes, charged down upon it. But Walakind kept the rest of us back. We left our horses and ran, shouting, yelling, swords drawn or axes whirling over our heads. Haimo and I managed to stay not too far apart. We killed or tried to kill. We saw blood jumping, we screamed and we struck. After a time — which might have been a life-time or an hour — it suddenly appeared that there was no enemy, no Danes, and we were aching from head to foot.

We were close to a little stream and a pool and were beginning to feel the hurting of our cuts and bruises, not deep but sore enough. We drank from the pool.

Haimo pointed, "Look!"

There were the last of the Danes, straggling back towards the river, two of them nearby carrying a wounded man dripping blood. If we had felt stronger we might have chased them, perhaps made them drop their man for us to finish off. But already that was not what we wanted most.

"Finished!" I said.

We could now see people straggling out of the church where only a corner of the thatch had burned. We began to wash our wounds, but I had never in my life been so tired. All I wanted was to get my mail shirt off and lie on the ground.

My father appeared on his great horse which had something I did not wish to see hanging on his breast spike, and Walakind with him, both in a good mess but fine spirits. It was like the times when my father had been drinking at a feast, but before he was truly drunk — he shouted and gave great praises to both of us — as we stood there thick with mud and blood.

"We have won the battle, won it!" he shouted.

Then one of the men came, leading our two horses. Suelde whinnied, but winced as she smelled the blood on me. We took off our heavy mail coats.

I then asked Haimo had he seen Wolfin? He shook his head and we looked at one another.

We got on the horses and went to look. There was nothing around the pool, though we went up carefully, calling Wolfin's name, moving a little east where the small stream was only a trickle and there was a green tangle of flowers and moss and hazel bushes with the nuts hanging. It seemed for a moment a sweet-looking place. But — there were bodies there — and one of them was Wolfin. He was lying half over, his hand grasping at moss.

We dismounted quickly and tried to pick him up, but he whispered, "No, no," and I could see there was a great sword wound across his stomach and everything fallen out of him and dark blood pumping out. As we tried to move him he whispered, "No, no, leave me." His breath came shallow and his colour was going. He looked at us, trying to smile, but his face was turning greyish. He whispered, "My father... I go to my father..."

I knew what he meant and knew he was dying. I had a thought. I took off my iron hat and brought water quickly from the small stream, but it was clean and I spoke words over it, those words I had heard, bringing my mind back to the Abbey and all it had meant. I hurried back and poured a little over Wolfin's forehead, over the smudges of blood. He half-opened his eyes, looking at me, as I thought, sweetly. I said the words of baptism but in the noble tongue, yet he recognized my voice and my hand holding his. Perhaps he even knew that I had taken Hiltrud's little cross from round my neck and put it on his forehead. But too soon his eyes shut, his grip on my hand became nothing. He was dead.

"He is gone to his father," said Haimo.

"To Our Father."

"As you will," said Haimo. "But let us see that he is well buried."

I found two of the peasants and gave them the few bits of silver that I still had in my purse tucked under my leather coat. They said they would get my friend buried close to the church. I had to leave it to them, for my father and Walakind were shouting at us to come. And oh, I was tired. Suddenly. So tired.

Haimo had picked up the sword and axe which had been lent to Wolfin. There had been blood on both of them. It was all we could do to get onto our horses and stay in the saddle. Also, Haimo had taken the amber piece which was still hanging round Wolfin's neck. He gave it to me. Now, if even I look at it I fall to crying like a baby.

When at last we were back, after riding into Paris

across the bridges and through the great gates, with girls throwing flowers and the noise of cheering, I took off all my clothes and was given warm water to wash myself, Haimo helping me, until there was no more blood to stain the clean linen of my other shirt. By that time there was food and drink ready and waiting, but somehow I could not want to fill myself or even to join in the singing and shouting and laughing that was going on all round me. The Count's little daughter came over timidly with a garland of leaves and flowers. I bent down for her to put it on me, but I was glad she did not try to kiss me. And I kept thinking about Wolfin and where he would be now.

There was a great feast laid but I could not eat and the cuts and bruises began to hurt. Haimo told me afterwards that my father sent for me to be thanked by the Count of Paris, but I fell down and was excused and carried to bed. I only remembered waking in the morning, trying to untangle what had happened from what I had dreamed, and beginning to ask myself which way Wolfin's soul had flown and whether I had done right to it.

There was one good thing at least. The Lord against whom we had been sent had heard that the Danes had come and had rushed to our help, leading his men. They had perhaps turned the battle our way. So this Lord was thanked in words which were meant to show that he was loyal to the Count of Paris, and through him, King Louis, as though he had in fact taken the oath. Yet the man himself and his followers were well aware that no oath had been taken, and also that through seeing them fighting and doing great deeds, the Count would be wary of taking action against him, at least for a few years. Perhaps, indeed, his oath could be registered at the Royal Chancery by some other road.

I wished the same thing could have happened to my father, so that he too would not be oath-bound. But the Danes had come too late. At least it was now clearly time for us to go in all honour, once we had buried our own dead, two men only; not close friends, but it was sad for them to be lying here so far from home; and we had lost three horses.

There was little booty, for the Danish ships had got away before we could do anything and were now either out to sea and back to their own country or into some lands at the foot of the river where they had an armed camp set up and hard to attack. They had taken away most of their own dead, at least the ones who had worn gold.

There were a few weapons, mostly broken; my father was given a silver-hilted dagger, which he passed on later to my next brother. There were some presents for us from the Count: a handsome cup, some silver-handled table knives, and a box with a saint's picture, St. Genevieve I think, for me to take back to my mother; and also a piece of embroidered crimson silk, enough for a head veil. It must have come from very far away, perhaps even from beyond Byzantium and the other Empire, from the countries with the strange beasts which the Abbot had told me about, beyond the sun rising.

If you touched it with your cheek, this silk, it was as soft as a baby's hair. I hoped that my mother would not just put it away in her great chest. I wanted to see her wearing it.

Haimo had left a girl with child. She was gentle

and young and it was sad. She cried and kept pulling him down to kiss her. I was glad I had not let myself get entangled. It is a quick sweet, but trouble is sure to come. I gave him some money which he left for her, hoping she would find a husband. Perhaps it is best to go with a married woman if we must do this thing. It would be a great sin deserving a great penance, but also it could mean less pain. I do not think that Wolfin had ever had a girl even kiss him. He was only a Saxon hostage. But at least I had done what I could for him. Yet, had I the right, I, a sinful soul, myself awaiting judgement?

WE CAME back along the same rough roads between villages or forest paths, crossing the same rivers or marshes. Night came sooner, the leaves were turning

colour. Haimo and I were older, had done new things. I had fought in a tangle of anger and fear. Most likely I had killed. Or I might have been killed myself and never come home and I wondered if Suelde might have been killed if I had been careless or had broken my spear. It was good to feel her moving under my legs and smell the warm horse sweat.

At least the Count fed his horses well, and ours.

Above all I had escaped betrothal to the little princess. There had been whispers about next year, but next year was a long time on.

At last we were in our own forest. Haimo and I rode ahead and got a buck: it seemed to me that I was handling the hunting spear better than I used. It felt light after the war spear.

My father and Walakind had the liver from that buck, but they gave leave for Haimo and me to sit and share with them. They began to sing some of the old songs and although they had drunk all the wine by now, or else the little that was left had gone sour, the remembrance of the fighting seemed to be as good as wine to them and they went through it stroke by stroke, with great laughing. But I excused myself.

At last we were home, my mother welcoming us at the opened gate to the great yard, as she stood there, as I thought, beautiful. The lads rushed to take my father's bridle; he slid down heavily and threw his arms round her in a bear hug. I wondered what it meant to her, for it did not show on her face. She had not had news of us since the time Walakind had come back to raise the fighters, but one of the men had ridden hard to warn her an hour before that we were coming. So the table was set and we could smell the cooking.

Yet I could not sit down easily, nor could my father. All the time, after we had left the forest we had seen bad signs. He and Walakind looked at one another and swore into their beards. For although it had been a fair year for barley, the rye was patchy, half the crop it should have been, while the wheat had been struck by some kind of small plague, so that the heads turned black and it was clear there would be no good wheaten bread for our tables. Why? What had we done for God to punish us in this way?

I did not think it was any fault of the poor farmers and peasants. The Abbey crops were no better than the rest. It is hard to understand why these things should happen.

I said to my father: "What do we do? For now there will be so many needing our help."

Decent farmers and their wives were wondering if they had enough grain to keep them over winter and through to another harvest. These were the men and boys I had seen and talked with when they had sworn to my father on May Day, as free Franks, giving him protection as he gave it to them. It was his duty to help them and feed them if things went badly, as they would do for him. That oath-taking was always cheerful; there would be a great flow of beer, sometimes cakes; also, I think, dancing in the fields, but, because I was tied to the Abbey, I never took part, though my next brother, Ulric, sometimes did.

All this was bound to be in my father's mind. He looked at me hard. "You want to feed them?" he said. "What with?"

"Lord my Father," I said, "you got gold from the Count of Paris."

"Which you will find plenty of uses for when you are older," he answered.

"Perhaps there are many things which I shall not need," I said.

"You cannot escape being my heir," he said. "You

will have greedy-guts brothers and sisters who will need all I have! Yes, and will take it. Keep that in your head!"

He was becoming angry, red in the face. So I said no more, but on the first Sunday people kept on coming, some — and I was a little proud of this — first of all to me. Another thing which had made my father, and, for that matter, Walakind, angry, was that some of the hay had not been brought in the way it should have been. Whole swathes had been left out and rained on, so that it was spoiled, all for the want of a few hours' work. Some of those who should have seen to it were well beaten, not only slaves, but small freemen. It is a sin, not only against their Lord, but against a gift of God which had been wasted.

I was sad, too, about my little brother. One of my little sisters had died, but I scarcely knew her. It is hard on women to bear and suffer, but perhaps God sees that and is less strict with them than with men. Some of the monks, my teachers, say cruel things about women and their sins. But I know my own mother's sadness and goodness.

Ulric, my brother, was eager to hear of the battle. But it meant nothing to him, as it had meant nothing to me until so lately, that men were killed and killing. A boy always plays battles, but what are they? Perhaps after what I told him, he would understand a trifle more. Hiltrud was happy when I told her that I had worn her cross all the time, but I did not yet tell her where it had also been and had been left.

Should I then, take my so-well-known path to the Abbey? The last time I had been, as I knew now, a child. Now I was almost a man, with other burdens, of which a large one was this oath I had sworn to a man of whom I now thought little. So I thought to myself what I would say to my Abbot, tuning myself into the noble tongue as I walked under the lime trees, shuffling the fallen leaves. It was those in the Abbey who had taught and comforted me and had been my images of goodness.

I came to the door and they came hurrying and smiling in their monks' gowns, so gentle and friendly and unhurt by all that was now hurting me. They told me at once that my Abbot, who had been so long and so much my image of goodness and wisdom, was on pilgrimage to England of all places, that is Saxon England. But the Danes had begun attacking there too and had pillaged Abbeys and burnt towns.

There were true saints in England, and the King's courts were totally Christian. It was known that they were building churches and many of the free Lords could read and even speak a little of the noble tongue. I kept wondering whether these English Saxons were in any way like my Wolfin. Yes, my Wolfin — if God accepts me as his surety.

Somehow I had thought that all my old teachers at the Abbey would wish to see me and question me about what had happened and what I had been seeing and doing. It was, after all, my first real fighting, and my brother Ulric was keen enough to hear about it. Above all I had gone to the Abbey for counsel about what I had done — or perhaps not done — for Wolfin. But they seemed too busy to listen to me. They had their own difficulties and, it seemed to me now, their own little quarrels and differences.

There had been problems about the confraternity book. Two names had somehow been left out, so that they would not be known or prayed for in other monasteries. Yet, I wondered, would it matter so much? I had now seen death, which is different. Also their harvest had been as bad as everyone else's as far as the wheat went, so they must settle for rye bread and less beer. Like my father they had their free farmers to care for, as well as the crowd of cripples, old women and slaves who clung to anyone waiting at the gate.

When I was a young boy I used to like feeding them and being thanked and blessed, but now I wonder why God allows so many poor. At least the monastery has a good, sweet, drinking well, better than my father's. I stayed there for a few nights, speaking with my old teachers and helping where I could. It was a pleasure to be speaking all the time in the noble tongue. I had forgotten it a little, but soon it came back.

Back in our own great hall, however, I found my father angry, difficult to talk with, sometimes going back to muttered curses on the Count of Paris who had dragged him off when he should have been caring for his lands — as though he could have stopped whatever it was that had gone wrong with the wheat, though he would certainly have dealt better with the hay.

Haimo and I got together a few of the men so that we could make a hunt; this time I took Ulric my next brother, who had been with the monks during the summer, learning to read and write. I asked him to let me see his writing, but he did not want to show me; he had not liked his teaching. Nor had I at first, but I had always been able, God helping me, to see ahead. I had passed on to Ulric my own Latin grammar with my name in good Roman letters. It had been given to me by my aunt Adelheid and at that time I wished she had rather given me sweetmeats. I came to treasure it though, and even boast about it; the capital letters were done handsomely in red, and I was a little ashamed at my own scribbles here and there on the good vellum. At least Ulric was careful with it, and perhaps seeing the scribbles he would know that I was still partly a boy, nobody to be afraid of.

We had our hunting bows and Ulric managed to get a young deer, which we finished off. Then we got another, larger; but we did not see any wild pigs — the best meat. At least we had enough for everyone. My mother had plenty of herbs and there had been a great nut-gathering. There were apples and pears as well.

Then I told my sister what had come of the little cross she had given me. She began to cry. "Do you think your friend is in heaven now?" she asked me.

"I cannot but hope so," I said, "but surely not in hell." Yet I kept on thinking how Wolfin had muttered about his father, who was certainly not in heaven and had fought against and killed Christian Franks. Hiltrud was in no mood to think about hell. The man she was to marry had been killed in a fight with another of the small Lords, all over the pennies charged to people crossing a bridge he had put right after a flood. Not a big quarrel, and it should have been settled, yet he would not see reason. Could this have happened in the days of the Great Charles?

With his hand no longer over us, were we becoming less law-abiding?

This thought troubled me, but at least Hiltrud might get someone she liked better. She was pleased because she could now wear her dowry brooches and the crystal, hanging by little gold branches on the end of a chain, without thinking of the man she had not wanted.

My mother was pleased with the crimson silk and wore it for her Saint's Day. She had been busy since we left: first the washing and spinning of the wool from our sheep for the new hangings for the hall. People go behind them after eating, even the clergy, at least in winter when it is too cold in the yard and ours were now as filthy as a gutsy man's mind before confession. They had to be washed in the river as soon as the sun was warm enough to dry them, but some were beginning to fall apart and so my mother had boiled up the dye plants and dipped the yarn for the weaving; she had in mind a good criss-cross pattern. Without women we would have less colour in our houses. It should be said that now she had picked up at the summer market a slave woman, somewhat bruised-looking about the face, who said she was a weaver and knew just the pattern my mother wanted.

"Then why did they sell you?" my mother asked.

She said, "I had a baby."

"Whose?"

"My master's," she said, and then, "so she sold me."

That was clear enough and my mother also found, when she had the woman stripped, that she had been cruelly beaten. She worked well though and my mother told her that when she had finished the hangings she would be freed and married to a kind husband. The poor woman cried like a child because she had got little kindness in her life. These are sad stories but good when they come clean in the end. I wished I knew if my own would come clean.

I had hoped, when I was home again, that my dreams would go a better way. They were back now in force and always, always, something I knew I must do which I was stopped from doing. I would be fighting with devils and snakes and I would call to Wolfin to help me but there was no answer. Or else I knew that he was close and in trouble but I could not get near him. I would wake up in a sweat and not able to come clear at once. My mother gave me a drink of strong herbs to take at night and the dreams seemed less hurting but still they were there at my back.

And so the days went by; I was sad for the two children, mostly my little brother, and for my mother who had borne them and still kept a brave face, but women are used to sadness; perhaps it is their punishment for the fall of Eve...

Our people were still coming, in trouble, talking of how they would go hungry, and where was the seed corn for next year? No doubt things were not as bad as they said, but for sure there would be hard times coming. My father seemed angry and I kept out of his way.

One day, after a bout of shouting and swearing at everyone, he went off angrily, I was not sure where. I had to do the honours at table, in so far as I could. Two of the uncles had come over, as well as my aunt

Adelheid, the Abbess, asking me questions about the family of the Count, as well as saying that her wheat too, had failed and what was she to do. Someone must have told her about that proposed marriage with the Count's daughter and she scolded me for not making sure of it.

That was bad enough, but worse was to come. One of the uncles said to me, with the kind of laughing I did not like, that my father had left us to visit a certain woman. She had been left a widow with an estate as yet unclaimed. I said in anger that I knew this was not so, and prayed that I was right. The one good thing that my father had done before he left had been to hand over to me a gold and garnet cloak clasp which the Count had given him and to tell me to give it to the Abbey in thanks for our victory over the Danes and our safe return. "I do not want to have any gift of his about me," he had said.

So, as soon as I heard that my Abbot was safely back — and I was very glad that he had crossed the sea before the autumn storms — I rode across to the Abbey. I tethered Suelde at the gate and took in the clasp wrapped in a piece of linen. I knocked, noting that I had now no trouble in reaching the high hammer on the door. There was the smell of kitchen and soap and ground paint and now and then a little gust of incense. I went happily along the windy cloister, and happily my Abbot received me.

He asked first about the oath-taking. How had it gone? We spoke always in the noble tongue and it pleased me that he thought of me as a young man, not any longer a boy; if I stumbled over a word he put it gently into my mouth.

I told him first of the Abbey of St. Denis where we

had stayed; it pleased him to hear about his fellow Benedictines and the great works they were doing. Then I came to the oath, saying that it was certainly an oath of total fidelity to the young King Charles, chosen to rule by his father, the anointed King and Emperor, yet put through the Count of Paris. It was like drinking spring water from a dirty cup.

"The Count and other great nobles stand between us and our King," I said.

"And the Bishops?" he asked.

"It hurts me to speak so," I said, "but I believe that, as regards Paris, the Bishop is no better than the Count. As it happened he did not change sides with Count Gerard. But I understand that this was because of certain difficulties it would mean to himself. I heard too many whispers about the Bishop. Both he and the Count want power, not for the young King, the Protector of Christendom, but for themselves."

I think I must have spoken angrily, for my Abbot raised his hand to stop me, and I saw how all this was hurting him. "Yet the oaths," he said, "were solely to the King."

"Yes," I said, "for now. But made through those that our good King has appointed or whose position he and his councillors have verified — and he would find it hard to take their appointments away from them. From all I heard, the Lord Bishop of that diocese looks on it as his own hen-roost from which he takes all the eggs."

"So you think, my son," he said sadly, "that their power will increase? You think perhaps that the young King Charles in furthering the powers of the

Church — as is surely right thinking — may have been mistaken in the vassals he chose?"

I thought carefully how to answer, now that the Abbot was speaking to me not as a boy but as a man. At last I said, "I fear that this may be the sad truth. I can see a time ahead when the oath may be sworn, not to the King, but to the holder of immediate temporal power. My father thinks our lands are his because the great Charles gave them to his grandfather as a reward for his good service in war, which my father has continued. But now it is as though the lands were given by the Count and could, if there was excuse enough, revert to him."

My Abbot frowned; he stood up from his seat and walked to the small window, turning his back on me, I think so that I would not see his face. But when he turned he had put on a smile and said, "It may be that you are seeing this too darkly. I shall visit my friends at St. Denis and see what is their judgement on this Bishop. Surely, Abbot Hilduin had no part in this, and his successor Abbot Louis is a man of learning and probity. He has held great offices with no word against him, and he knows the workings of politics and where to put his trust. I believe and hope that he has more power than many Counts, and, above all, he is obedient to his own rules, which have power throughout Christendom. If the great company of the Benedictines were to suspect ill doings -" He shook his head. I hoped very much that he was right.

Then I asked, "Could an oath be invalid if it does not match the reality which is intended by the swearer?"

He frowned and shook his head, "It is not so easy. An oath is an oath. If a man breaks his oath to a superior, then those who have sworn to him may also, in turn, break their oaths. And so the whole fabric of Christendom would be in danger. Who are we to judge the validity of an oath? But to think that the Franks have fallen so far — no, it is beyond me. I fear from what you tell me that the Bishop is not doing God's work but his own. How can any King rule well if those on whose behalf he is ruling — and I mean we, the Dioceses and the Clergy of Frank-land — pay no heed or loyalty to him? If the oath to him has been diminished into an oath to them — this surely is the end of Kingship!"

A terrible sadness came on the Abbot, and so, to take his mind away from this pain I asked him about England. How was it?

He cheered at this and began to tell me of the Christian Kings and how they were holding most of England against the Danes. The armies of Wessex and Mercia, which is to say Saxon England, though there is also Northumbria and perhaps other kingdoms, were keeping a strict watch and saw to it that the Danes did not meddle with the poor Christians, who were still able to live and worship under the Danish occupation.

"Did you yourself meet the Saxon Kings and Bishops, dear Father?" I asked.

"Of course. For I was at the Court of King Aethelwulf of Wessex and spoke with him and his fine young sons. He is as devout a man as one in his station of life can be. It seemed a happy and prosperous household, but always with fear of the Danes at the back. The King himself was a pupil at

Winchester, where Swithun, whom I knew a little, was Bishop. But the King's Latin was no better than yours!" And he smiled warmly at me. He went on, "There is constant trouble with the Danes, landing along the eastern and southern coasts of England. Well, you know the Danes by now, in your sword hand. Over there they have taken their evil ships into the Thames, which is the king-river of England. They slaughtered and burnt in Mercia, the neighbour kingdom to Wessex, and razed houses and churches in Canterbury and London, doing much harm."

The same enemy. The same cruelty.

My Abbot went on, "King Aethelwulf is constantly sending out his men, though indeed every earl takes it on himself to raise men from his shire against the Danes. Still, the Church is strong and there is much building of churches and monasteries. I stayed in Winchester myself. King Aethelwulf intends to go on a pilgrimage so I offered him hospitality here should they ever pass through our lands. Yes, I thought very well of the Saxons in England."

Saxons. Perhaps this was the time to ask my question.

I said, "I had a Saxon friend who was killed fighting the Danes and has left me with a sore question. May I speak of it?"

In some surprise my Abbot said, "Surely." And then, "You have tears in your eyes, my child. Why?"

So I told him everything, down to the very words of baptism, which I knew because I had listened to them often and seriously, and which I had used myself in the knowledge that even a layman can use them in time of desperate emergency, as when a new-born baby is at death's door. But I did not hide the fact that Wolfin had been torn away from his dead father and baptised, but had neither asked for it nor agreed, as had so many of the conquered Saxons, and had not accepted it in his soul. As I was watching my Abbot's face I could see, when I told him this that he frowned and that his mouth was working a little.

"Having been given this gift, this pearl beyond price, he threw it away. Of his own will. You understand that?" he said.

"I know indeed, my father," I answered, "and spoke to him more than once. I told him it was the greatest gift man could give to man, I told him it was the way to heaven. I took him into churches, had him listening to services. I told him about the saints. I told him also about hell. Yet he could not accept it. Although I think he loved me a little."

"Did you speak clearly?"

"Yes, and often," I said, "of the infinite joys of heaven and how we would meet there. But all he would say was that unless his own father was there he would not want a glimpse of it. His father most surely died a heathen and yet my friend — he spoke of the idol of the Saxons, his idol, not perhaps that he believed in it — truly I do not think that, but it was the sign of his people. And he was alone and unhappy."

"So, you gave him Christian compassion and because of that you have come nearer to God, but you could not save his soul."

"Yet in the end—" I said, for I could not bear to think that in the end what I had done was not sufficient.

"If he knew what you were doing and agreed to it and repented of all his sins, which must have been many—"

"But he was dying! There was no time for repentance. He only knew that I was with him, his friend."

"He should have repented," said my Abbot, sadly I thought. "Above all for refusing to admit his wickedness, his deep error in not accepting his baptism, even though it was by force."

I did not know what to say. I felt bruised. At last I said, and I think there were tears coming down my cheeks: "Can I not take this burden on myself? I can make a pilgrimage. I can take vows—" I could not finish what I meant to say. I felt choked.

But my Abbot shook his head. "No. You were a good friend. But this was beyond your reach. Now, my child, it is over. Do not think about it. You too have many duties. You are your good Lord Father's eldest son and he counts on you. Go back to him now."

I could not speak. I bowed my head to his blessing, but I did not hear it nor feel it. I stumbled out, and looked for Suelde. Haimo was there; I told him what the Abbot had said. And it seemed to me that I no longer felt as I used to do, that the Abbot meant everything to me, that he was my spiritual parent. No, never any more.

Haimo put his arm round my neck. "You and I know," he said, "whatever they say in there, that Wolfin is no more in hell than we are, and we are all three going to meet again. They think they rule us, but, under God, our souls are our own."

"Haimo," I said, "I think with part of me that you are right. And perhaps in there they have tied themselves to a pattern which most certainly came from God, but has had nails put in it so that it cannot move." And Haimo laughed and gave me an apple.

Yes, I was comforted a little as I bit into the apple, more by the feel of his arm round my neck than by what he said. But I ask myself, over and over, which could be right? I shuddered inside myself to think of Wolfin in hell where I could not reach to save him. It is a terrible thing not to have total belief in what one is told by those who should know, those in authority, above all those for whom one had deep love and trust. Oh, it is like coming out of the house on a bitter cold day and knowing one has to make a path through the woods. It is, perhaps, becoming a man.

Yet, I must find a way. Perhaps, if I read the scriptures again and again, I might, by myself, find something, a grain of mustard seed — to tell me that Wolfin was at peace, that what Haimo had said was God's truth.

We rode back together. Suelde was beginning to grow her winter coat.

And then, when we came back, there was my father with a load of corn, of good wheat, in baskets and woven sacks, and there in front of him was a small crowd of our men, some with their wives. I came through and saw that he was giving out the corn; it had come from higher ground where, it seemed, the plague had not struck. And I saw, in the waggon that had brought it in, the pieces of gold that the Count had sent with his first message, bidding him come for the oath. I looked at my father.

"Must get it out of my house," he said to me gruffly. I knew what he meant. And I was glad to my heart that this was what he had gone for and not what I had half feared.

He went on giving out the corn, household by household. "These are my men," he said, "on land that the great Charles gave to my grandfather and to me. My grandfather swore to him in the name of all his fighters, their wives and children. They have sworn to me." And he glared at me.

"At least," I said, "I did not marry the Count's kitten." And then he laughed and slapped me on the back and made the kind of joke about marriage that Haimo might have made. And I watched the faces of the men and women who were taking away the good wheat, seed corn and milling corn, not enough to see them through — we would all be on rye bread and porridge — but at least they would have good white bread for Christmas.

PART TWO

CHAPTER ONE

YET that Christmas and the months that followed it, were, as I came to know too well, the last of my years of innocence. For indeed I am more than a little changed from the young man who felt secure in that guidance of the Church and the sense of being a free Frank with goodwill towards other Franks, soaked like wine on bread in the remembrance of the great Charles and the deeds of his followers.

Yet I did not understand at first that there was any change coming. For another two long years I stayed mostly at home and came closer than I had been to my brother Ulric and also, for a time, to Hiltrud my sister. It was through her that I came nearer to the understanding of what a woman might wish for in her life. She may know that things are going badly, but it is hard for her to go out into the world of war, the hard lies and the treachery, in which, sadly enough, we must all find our way. And in this world a woman is often enough used as a snare, but is also the victim. In the end Hiltrud accepted a suitor, who was at least more to her liking than the one who had made her so unhappy at first. Indeed she left the house merrily enough.

I took over much of my father's burden over petty things and began to know how to judge people, which was the voice of lying and which that of truth. There were two bad seasons and hungry months before the harvests, with decent folk walking the roads for bread. But then came a fair harvest and we were all glad of it. I was less at the Abbey, but I saw to it that my brother Ulric studied hard and was now, with some pleasure, using my own books.

At first I was jealous of his doing this, then, quite suddenly I did not care about the books, and instead had the great pleasure of speaking together with him in the noble tongue. Earlier, if it had been a choice of which of us sons would finish the story of his life within the cloisters of the Abbey, I would have been happy to be the chosen one. But that was no longer so. I still respected my Abbot and in a way loved him as I had done as a child, but now there seemed to be two ways to choose from, and I knew in my heart that I must make my own choice, not his.

It was not the first spring, but the second, and there had been days of fair weather and small flowers seemed to dance about along the forest edges, when word came that the Danes were attacking again. It was the villages along the Seine that were suffering once again. I had put in much practice with sword and spear and so had Haimo. Just once or twice I thought of Wolfin and if only there had been the three of us, it would have been a merry time.

So a good troop of us, led by my father, rode as hard as the horses could take us along with the Count's messenger who had come for us, one of the court whom I had met earlier. We met in with a great company, truly a Frankish host, all quarrels forgot. We must strike quick and hard. And so we charged into the Danes, catching them when they least expected. I speared one in the throat and the blood splashed down, well to his knees as he began to fall. We remember our first killings.

We did not go back to Paris. The Count would hear of our deeds and indeed he sent messages of thanks and hopes of seeing us again at his court. He remembered me with a gift of a handsome buckle set with garnets. But none of us wanted to go there, unless perhaps Haimo, who sometimes, as I knew, thought of the girl he had got with child. And once or twice I wondered if the little princess had been married off.

So that was all. My father had a cut on his leg, which we bandaged up; when we got back my mother put herbs on it and in a while it was healed. A true man will have many such a marking, though I was pleased enough to have little but bruises. We asked ourselves how soon were the Danes likely to come back, for it seemed they would try to seize on such bits of our coastland as were not well defended. My father and I went together to the Abbey to be cleared of our killings, although we knew they were not sinful and indeed there was a service of gratitude and rejoicing at the fall of our enemy who was also God's. It seemed that my Abbot wished to take me aside and speak with me, yet somehow I no longer wanted this — although once I would have wished for it above all, for it would have been a true cleansing. He told me, though, that he had been sent a letter by an old friend, who was writing a history. But at the time I did not even listen to the name, so far apart had we become.

There was another thing. That summer I went with Haimo to one of the great Fairs. These would be held here and there. Merchants came with goods from far away, from beyond Frank-land, either from across the seas or else sometimes from Spain, where the strong, heathen Saracens are masters of all arts. There were sword blades more beautiful than any I had ever seen but the price of the best was away beyond me. Our main concern was that my father's great horse had become too old to cover a lively mare as he once did, or to charge or swerve quick as a bird at my father's toe-touch. I was told to buy a certain horse he had heard of, if the price was right. I found this horse he had heard about and there was hard bargaining which ended with drinking. And that in turn ended in a violent need for what I had so far, though not without prayer and fasting, kept at arms length away from me.

In the morning when I woke Haimo was laughing at me, but said that I had indeed picked a right peach and done well by it.

"But if — " I said, for indeed I had no wish for marriage and such.

"No, no!" said Haimo. "If that thing was done by you that I expect she truly wished for, there will be no trouble with her father. I will see to it."

"But she — " I began.

"She was no wife for you," said Haimo, "and nobody saw."

I remember a certain fear inside myself and I said, "Yet God has seen."

"It is something that God has seen often enough," said Haimo, "and all of His doing for pulling that sweet rib out of father Adam."

So it went; there was no trouble. Yet, I thought to myself, I am in some way changed, and I remembered how I had killed that Dane on the edge of the river, or perhaps killed, for I was never truly sure that it was I who had given the death stroke, although I had boasted of it. I knew that I must learn to kill with certainty and take as little heed to it or remembrance of it as I had done with the sweet girl who had wriggled under me. So we left the Fairgrounds, leading the new great horse, who was already well trained for war, with a good reputation, and he gave us no trouble.

I was a little sorry for the old horse whom I knew well, but he was put out to grass which was plentiful enough. And it seemed that now I must have a horse bigger than Suelde if I was to go off on a killing venture, such as I had heard about and even read about, for now surely I had proved myself a grown man. Yet Suelde could still carry me well enough, so I need not yet come to a quick decision. I spoke about this to my father, and he asked if I had looked lately at the three-year-old which his old horse had got on the mare we called Duck because of the way she slid into the pond water and us laughing. Yes, but the three-year-old was untrained and I was impatient. I knew that Suelde, by understanding so well what I wanted of her, would serve me best. I wondered if this was some way the same as a man thinking about his wife.

It was becoming clear to me therefore that I must seize on a life of my own. If I stayed at home there would be too much of the day-to-day burden, more and more of my father's, necessary but trivial, with little room for honour and glory. It began to seem that those were the great aims for a man and I must follow them. In a way my father understood and only asked that when these were achieved I would come back and take his place.

First I must go over to the Abbey and go through my penances for a long list of wrong-doings and wrong thoughts which had got their claws into my soul. I knew this, but did not feel myself cleansed, either by prayer or by fasting, as I had hoped would come to pass. I tried to speak of this to my Abbot, but it seemed to me that because he himself had never felt my temptations he could not help me to master them. What he did was to give me almost a dozen carefully written letters to friends in the great Benedictine Abbeys, lamenting all the killings that were happening between those who had power and wished for more, all through Frankland. And sorrow it was for the two kings, Charles and Lothar, both of them grandsons of the Great Charles. For which should a man follow, as surely I could count myself a man?

It seemed that, for my father, it was most certainly Charles, that one who later was called the Bald, but in those days had hair in plenty and a fine shining beard. Yet handsome is as handsome does. My father and mother gave me a string of names to remember with some special message or token for each. They did not want me to leave them, but understood that it had to be.

So what now of my oath to the Count of Paris? There had been no word from him, calling us back to Paris. Once there had come a party to visit us, which had both clerics and men of standing and to whom we gave careful entertainment and gifts (that they chose), mostly great sacks of wheat and barley — for now God had smiled on us and we had reaped a better harvest. They also took some young cattle. Ulric kept somewhat away from them, a little unsure of his Latin, but they spoke to him about the pleasures of the Count's court. This he set against what I had told him, and so he was wise enough to say that he must finish his education.

It was clear enough that they dangled the pleasures of the court in front of me too, and I feared that I would get myself entangled there. Above all I wished to be free, for surely freedom is always the first step towards making a choice. There was at least opportunity enough. I asked myself what would the great Charles have thought of this warring between his grandsons, the promises broken almost before they were written out and the commoner people, their small lands and themselves, bargained with as though they were toys.

All the time, beyond our own land, there were the Danes ravaging along the north, and stranger, yet more fearsome folk behind them, beyond the dark forests to the east of Frankish lands.

And another thing: to our westward and south,

there were still the Saracens who did not acknowledge God and the saints, but only their own god or
god-maker who was, I had heard, called Alla or some
such. They held the places of the Bible, all the
ground that our Jesus had trodden, which must
somehow be taken back into Christian hands. Yet
they had marvellously beautiful swords and jewels
and it was said that their women were the most
beautiful in the world and gave more pleasure to a
man.

All this was in my mind when I set out, on a
spring morning, waving goodbye to my mother. She
was anxious for Hiltrud who was now with child, yet
seemed to be in good cheer with a husband she liked
well enough. Now there would be some little space
before the next sister was ready, who, I thought, was
no beauty, but gentle and with a good humour. Ulric
was in a gloom, envying me, as he was bound to do.
But I myself had shaken off my family, at least in my
mind.

SO WE LEFT

our homes merrily enough, Haimo and I and the free lads who had come with us, laughing and telling jokes. We went south and east through the green forest, crossing rivers at the ferries and keeping a good distance from the coast where we might fall into Danish camps. Here we could always find water and grazing, and green sprouts as a salad for our meat when one of us had been lucky with his bow. It became clear that, as we came on

a village or a good house, the people there felt themselves threatened by armed men, but when I spoke courteously, doffing my hat and assuring them that we had come in peace, we were mostly made welcome; for, after all, a stranger coming is like a little new light in a dark house.

So we gave news and also received it, for that is how the world goes. They would ask, cautiously, whom we favoured in the struggles for rule and power that were forever going on. Sometimes we would find a monastery or be guided to one, and I might be shown the books and other treasures, which was to me a great pleasure. Indeed it could be a pleasure also to the monks to have such possessions admired and praised and to get such news as I myself could give, all in good Latin speech. Soon enough, it became clear to me that if I and my party — small but well-armed — were to offer our services to one or another of the groups who were fighting, we would be well paid and treated and might, with luck, win a few good prizes. Best if we could fall in with strong allies of King Charles, but if there were other quarrels afoot we might take sides. And this was how it went all that summer.

At first, if we did no good, at least we did no harm. We were pleased with ourselves, or, if I were not in good heart, Haimo would joke with me and the sky would clear. All of us had some kind of armour, though the heaviest would be on the pack horses, and each carried sword and hunting spear. I had seen to it that Haimo's sword was no worse than mine, though sometimes I thought that one day I would have one of the saracen blades. Between us, we knew as many songs as leaves on a tree. I had my letters from the Abbot and messages from my parents, but I trusted more to my own tongue.

We met with other small bands, like ourselves, for there were many young men for whom small wars were great sport. Like myself, they had parents who had given them good horses and good armour, though sometimes of an oldish pattern. Often they called themselves by bigger names than they had rights to and claimed great doings with women which were far enough from the truth. So what were we all about? There was one thing certain. Although we could go through forms of words, we had totally forgotten God. But God had not forgotten us.

I am deep ashamed now, to think how we and many others rode out, boasting and ready for anything, and to think of what it led to. I hardly know how many months we spent in folly and destruction. There were some like myself, who had some learning and indeed respect for those who had been our parents and teachers and we would use Latin, partly to put ourselves beyond the common crowd. But there was impatience in the air. What suited us best was to find a good family, ready to teach its neighbours a lesson, perhaps in the name of King Charles or perhaps the Count or some other great name. There would be much shouting and charging, but not too many deaths, only cuts and bruises and the gross satisfaction of power.

We would come to an Abbey and a great house beside it, perhaps with one of its members as Abbot, host and controller. But if we went to the guest rooms in the Abbey we were bound in courtesy to join in the services, as well as going to Confession and taking the consequences. That did not suit us, although I still took great pleasure in the sight of a treasure of gold or silver-work or a splendidly illustrated psalter. Better, we thought, to stay in the house, perhaps with less comfort and dropping our

Latin, but with the chance of finding an easy girl or older woman, to do what we wished with and never to see again. And best of all, if there was a quarrel, we would join in and perhaps come back with a helping of booty.

Sometimes we were in true combat, out to smash down those we called our enemy. Blood would be shed, riders on the ground, screams and yells and fierce neighings. I myself only suffered a few scratches and nor do I think we did any real killing, though we might well grab a prisoner for exchange. The end seemed always to be shouting and pleasure.

In time of wars (and do they ever cease totally?) small wandering bands like ours might be found everywhere in the Frankish kingdoms. There was always an excuse for arms, and that meant killing. I suffered nights when I lay awake wondering whether this had always been so, and whether, if the great Charles had been still living, it would all have been stopped. And would that be what I wanted? Peace? What would I do with it?

Some of the wandering young warriors thought they could do great deeds and make themselves feared and powerful. They had to find enemies to smash down and would then twist words in the scriptures into whatever they wished for. Yes, I could do that myself and felt a certain shame, and yet I carried on with it. I could see Haimo's face twisted into a grin and knew he was despising me a little, though he would never admit to it.

We often changed direction, putting off the time when we might be called on by King Charles, so there could be another adventure, another band like ourselves that we had heard of and with whom we might have a mock battle — or even a real one, if things went badly at our meeting. Or it might be a single armed man, or more likely boy, who would join with us. Older men had mostly got themselves past this game or had been killed or else lost a leg or fingers or had their faces ruined. Sometimes I saw all this clearly and wondered if it had been the same in the days of the Great Charles — or was it partly to do with the quarrels between the leaders and above all between those with the blood of the Great Charles?

We were pleased enough to offer our services to those with quarrels and were likely to come well enough out of it. We would take vows of friendship with one group, then another. It scarcely mattered. But I was the one who made such decisions and Haimo, grinning, would tell me I was going the right way. I was my father's son. And I wondered just how he was mocking me, since he also was my father's son.

I had used two of my Abbot's letters, but not the others. It seemed to me that I no longer felt the old sense of security, not so much of the body as of the soul, when I felt the walls of a monastery, or even a little wooden church, closing around me. I would make the right gestures and answers, but, as it were, not from my true self. I could become suddenly in great fear of the Last Day and the resurrection of the dead, among them those I had killed or seen killed and some who had been refused burial.

I could not bring myself to speak of these fears to one who was a true pillar of the church. Surely they might cast blame upon me which I knew I deserved. One of the letters was to the Confessor of a woman, a lady of high degree no doubt, but what would he or she know of my soul-sickness?

So the days went by. Yet one evil thing stands out beyond the rest. Only, when I try to think of it, or speak about it, all goes into a dark blur... All I remember is charging — but why? — into a cluster of huts, poor forest people, charcoal burners perhaps, for there was a fire. Dear God, there was a fire! Then the sharp whinnying, the dog that leapt at Suelde's neck and my own hand slashing down. A stone thrown. And then. I cannot remember. I do not know what lit all that anger in me, why I let go, not only of mercy but of decency. They must have offended me. Words, words. I have dreams some times, of the evil coming back, swamping me and a voice saying, That will teach them how to speak to their betters. Laughing. Myself laughing, shouting, slashing, full of hell's wine. I only remember catching a running man, taking his head off, and Haimo looking at me as though I had hurt him. Then again, Haimo shouting at me, did I know what I had done, the children, the little maid... And there was the fire blazing.

And then, yes, then I remembered something, yes, I knew it too well, and yet it seemed to be not me. I had set spurs into Suelde, but Suelde gave a sideways start and there were bodies and the smell of blood, yes, and burnt flesh and a screaming that followed me, that follows me still, that comes at night until I am fully awake and on my knees. Death in battle is one thing. But there was *no battle*. Only killing. Only blind, hideous killing. And blind shame.

Suelde was bleeding from the neck — that had set me off... But it was not a heavy cut. I had looked at it — it turned into the cut I had made on — who,

112

which?

I had hardened myself not to speak to Haimo and I saw that he was avoiding me. That was what hurt. Later, when I understood what had happened (and seen myself going down into a deep pit of hell) I found out that he had tried to hold my hand, to stop me from murder, but I had hit him across the face; indeed there were the bruises. My Haimo, to whom I had thought myself superior. Haimo who went back and found two poor women, half-mad, trying to bury what was left. He had helped them, not saying he had been one of the attackers, and given them all the money he had.

My doing had shamed him and my men, the others who had followed me, and I felt that there was an end to the old trust and good cheer. We had been insulted, I explained, and were in danger, but they did not believe me. It was after this that they began to go their own ways or back to their homes, with what small booty they had, and surely, bad memories.

Perhaps the worst part was that a few days after this we came to a certain abbey and I prepared myself for a painful cleansing. Yet when I came to speak of it in my confession — and I believe I was even sobbing a little — it seemed to shrivel. It was taken lightly as something that a brisk young man does in folly and that repentance will wipe out. But I knew better. I knew that it could never be wiped out. Never. It was written for all time in hell's book. There I would meet it.

Yet, more to regain Haimo's respect and love, I went dutifully through all the penances, not only those that I had been given, but those that I chose myself. I watched and prayed throughout cold nights, for it was now autumn. I wore a shirt of nettles, ate no meat, drank no ale or wine. Haimo felt that he shared some of this, saying gruffly that he could have stopped me. But was that possible when I had totally let go to evil? I wondered then and I still wonder, could I be forgiven, not, surely, by those I had injured, but perhaps in the end by God's mercy?

And what now? Our cheerful company was leaving me. Should I go back? No, I thought, never (or nearly never, for what is never when one is still young?) I prayed and begged for a sign. I sat among the tombs in the yard of that monastery. I hated myself there for being alive. I hated the Abbot who had not punished me, who would not see how deeply I had sinned. The monks loved me in as far as they could reach to me and I loved no-one. It was dead in me. Then Haimo came. "We are going," he said, "you and I. Perhaps God will send us a sign."

"I cannot look for it," I said.

"Not yet," he said, "but I can."

He brought Suelde out and she nestled against me, hoping for an apple. She was only a beast but better than I, and not weighted by sin. I remember there was a sudden storm and I thought the lightning was sent to strike me. I had begun to feel a certainty that whatever happened in the natural world was as it were pointed at me and I could not yet see that this was a kind of vanity, a sin in itself.

It seemed that there was now a thin bridging of peace between the two Kings, Charles and Lothar, who had met at Verdun; but who could be sure, for kings feel themselves above oaths? Yet oaths had been taken, prisoners freed, much coming and going and bartering of lands between Counts and Margraves and such, and little heed for what those below them might have wished. Not a few of the lay-abbots, of whom there were many, had sure seats in the temple of Mammon. At the time, however, nothing was clear and sometimes I felt a sadness that was half-laughing for those heads of families who were unsure which way the weathercock was turning.

We were now heading south. Haimo knew this was away from home, and from all he knew and loved, but he said nothing and quieted the lad who was still with us, riding one of the pack horses. I think he understood that I was in some way trying to escape from myself.

I had given Haimo a gold chain which my mother had given me in the days when I was still mostly innocent and as the need arose he would take a ring from it and buy food and beds for ourselves and fodder for our patient beasts. Mostly we would find an abbey with cells for guests and a table with simple dishes and clear water. Sometimes I would spend a whole night kneeling in some dark chapel, hoping to feel a touch of forgiveness and yet not daring to expect it. I would sometimes say to myself that worse things had been done often enough, but that made my own guilt no less.

And now, as we rode further south and felt the sun still warm, even so late in the year, I felt I was among changes. First, there was the natural world, clad in a difference, for here the trees and plants were different and even the small birds had different notes from ours. The great trees bore chestnuts which we sometimes ate, buying them for pennies in the market; I had liked them above all when I was a child and they were brought into the house once or twice in the year, yet here they grew everywhere and were thought of as peasant food.

Also, as we went further south, there were the olive trees, seeming more grey than green, and gnarled; their oil was precious in our own lands, but here it was used for cooking. There were many vineyards too; they had borne fruit and were now being cut hard back, but there were still a few grapes and sometimes fresh grape-raisins. All this was pleasing, and yet it could not heal the constant thought of my sins, for indeed I now looked back, not only to the last killing, but to all the folly and wickedness that we had laughed at and admired.

This country, called Septimania, was in a sense under the rule of King Charles, but there were many who only spoke of Pippin of Aquitaine, to whom they looked as their lord. Nor was it sure whether Pippin was a true vassal of King Charles, for indeed, in this country, nobody even swore by his name, but only by Pippin's, so that I was careful in my own speech.

There were many small hills, and almost every one seemed to have a village or small town on it, with at least a castle and a church or more, with a strong wall all round, and a gate where we might be greeted civilly or looked at with suspicion or hate. Most of the folk were friendly enough, though their speech was hard to make out. When we came to a church or monastery, all was easy and in the noble language.

There were ruins which had even been left by the old Romans. They had high pillars which stood even if the roof had fallen in. Some, I thought, must be temples of the heathen Gods, but had doubtless passed into good Christian hands. There was marble aplenty which seemed to shine in the sun. I saw a marble piece with a face on it, perhaps a Roman God from the pagan days. It lay on a sunny bank, and Haimo and I threw stones at it while the horses found some grazing. I remember we broke its nose and I thought, So perish all heathen things. All that is against the Lord and his instructions.

After questioning we found ourselves to be near to the monastery of Gellone, which had seemed, when my Abbot gave me his letter, to be so far as not to be reached. Yet here it was, though I did not yet know what its meaning would be to me. One thing was certain. This was part of the kingdom of my lord, King Charles, but he was far away and it was clear to me that his name meant little here, for the common folk knew only their old leaders, who were loyal enough for the most part. So I must approach carefully with my Abbot's letter. This one I was determined to give, though I was not sure why, only that the man might have a different relationship with God.

He was, I knew, not an abbot but a man of great power and influence, as the confessor and friend of the Lady Dhuoda. Now this lady, herself from a noble family, was married to Bernard of Septimania, which is to say all these fertile lands through which we had of late been travelling, and whose folk seemed to be prosperous and in good heart, with wealth and merchandise in the small towns and a well-fed people in the small villages. The Lord Bernard, as I heard, was but seldom at his great house, or rather castle, for indeed it was strongly built, and the outer walls took in the whole of the hill of Uzès and the town and the Abbey of Gellone, so that it was, as it were, a small country which must be governed by one hand.

It was said — and this became clearer with every day I was there — that this Lord Bernard favoured life at the King's court in Aachen, where he had a great position as well as some doubtful pleasures which he found there and which were whispered in my ear, though I could scarcely believe them. Certainly he had taken away his two sons, one being William who was near my own age and the other a mere babe whom he had got on his wife during a brief visit and then snatched away to have in his own safe keeping, so that its sad mother never knew even what name had been given to him.

This seemed to me to be a terrible hurt for any man to do to a woman, let alone his faithful wife, and there was never any word against the Lady Dhuoda, whom he certainly entrusted with his estate even if not with her own children. She had good advisers, especially from the monastery, but the final decisions were hers. All the time I was there I heard nothing but praise for her patience and judgment and also for her sense of mercy. When she held court in the great hall and heard witnesses, there was always a sense of emptiness there and I was sad for this so heavily-burdened lady and asked myself often how could her husband have so fallen as to leave her in this way, childless, when she had, as I was told, followed him on dangerous campaigns during the year after their marriage.

Yet this same Lord Bernard had done great deeds.

He had kept the Spanish March, so that there had been no threats or attacks, either from the old March kingdom, or from the Saracens beyond. It was said — and in Uzès I seemed to move among tale-tellers — that he had his enemies in Aachen, which might well be true. It also seemed that at one time he and the Lord Pippin had come together and indeed I heard so many conflicting stories about him that I can only say that some must be false. It was his father, who had been a warrior and keeper of the March and held the greatest post in Frank-land and who came finally as a monk in his old age and died here in the monastery of Gellone, which he had built, with his sins doubtless washed clean. They showed me the plain tomb slab he had asked for.

The letter from my Abbot was given to Brother Milo, the Confessor, of whom, clearly they were in some awe. They told me that I must call him simply Brother, which, I felt, was partly true humility and partly a kind of spiritual pride. He appeared happy to receive the letter, spoke with warmth of my Abbot, and asked me how things were going for him. Then we were given a sleeping-room and stable-room and he took me to his library, speaking with a kind of mock modesty of the many books, some very beautiful.

He showed me the cell where William, the founder, father of the present ruler Bernard, had lived and died. Yet, I thought to myself, he must have been a slaughterer, without mercy, for that is how wars are won, just as unkindly towards our fellow Franks as against the Saracens and Jews who have taken the worldly Jerusalem from us, though they can never take the Jerusalem of our souls. So where is William the founder? If safe in heaven he must be totally changed. Is that possible? If so, what must I now try to become?

All this went through my head while I was explaining myself to Brother Milo. I also much admired the garden which had many useful plants of which I had heard but never seen. I told him some of my troubles and asked that he would give me a hard penance, to wipe out some of my many sins. The next day he told me that the Lady Dhuoda would give me audience and added that she was skilled in the kind of advice which might help a young man. He went on, "I have told her the history of your sins and your penitence," and looked at me hard.

So I combed my hair and Haimo cut it so that it fell even, and I put on the least worn of my shirts, and my soft leather tunic with gilt buttons. He teased me a little, as I remember. He was to come with me as far as the curtain which was hung between the great empty hall and the Lady Dhuoda's retiring room. It was woven with leaping deer and fruiting trees.

She called me to come in, which I did and offered as many courtesies as I could. I had, I suppose, expected a woman older than my mother, but she seemed younger rather than older, though of a marked dignity and even sadness, and wearing one ring with a great sapphire set in gold. I think her kerchief might have been silk, had I dared to touch it.

She motioned me to sit on a stool beside her and said, speaking still in the noble tongue, "You have come from the north, young man?"

I answered that indeed I had and she sighed,

saying, "The oak forests — you know them? — and the broad, slow rivers."

"Yet here, noble Lady," I said, "you have vines and olives and that great, blue sea."

Then I had a thought that perhaps she was indeed far from the places of her girlhood, where she must have been happy, with little chance of return, and so her days of happiness were far away, and all that remained was a painful courage and a long waiting. So I said quickly that I too loved the oak forests of the north but perhaps, because of my sins, I had made my goodbye for ever. Thus we spoke together for a little and I felt I would do anything in the world to recover her happiness. Suddenly she pointed to the desk where there was a strip of writing. She said, "This will be for my son, William; I hope to guide him a little over the keeping of faith. He is not yet as old as you are. Will he understand?"

"Surely," I said, "for this is almost the first thing to be learnt." And I remembered my talk with my father, long ago it seemed, about keeping faith.

She sighed a little, "It is so long since I have even seen him. I do not know..." And she shook her head. But then she took a straight look at me and said: "I have heard of your penance, young sir, which you deserved, but now that must end and you must come back into the world. Your nettle shirt — it smells," and she gestured to me: "Take it off."

I would have retired to do as she said — or rather ordered — but she said, "No. Here."

So I took off my tunic and my linen shirt and then the nettle shirt which I had grown almost used to since the nettles lost their sting. I stood awkwardly.

121

Indeed the shirt had become stinking. She looked me up and down and I felt myself blushing. But she nodded. "Tell me," she said, "What are your intentions?"

"I want," I said, "to become wholly clean. In my soul."

I could see she was laughing a little at me.

"What is the worst thing you have done?" she asked.

For a moment I could not speak. Then I told her, but somehow not in the way I had spoken at confession — more, as it were, a pouring out of blood and dirt. She listened and then shook her head.

"What is done is done," she said. "Nobody can change it. Not even God. All your life it will be a dark shadow. That is your punishment. Yet in the end you may come out of it. As many have done in past years such as my own husband's father, for I do not doubt that he is now truly a saint. So. Put your shirt on again... No! not the nettles. That is a child's game. I shall give you a balm to lay on. Do you have a servant?"

I thought of Haimo. "I have a friend," I said, "who cares for me and sometimes chides me. And a boy for my horse."

"Well, well," she said. "Your friend can lay on the balm." And then, slowly and carefully and looking me full in the face, so that I almost flinched as from a hard light, "I will send you on an errand." She added, "Into another world. Across the March."

CHAPTER THREE

IT WAS

a few days before I was to see her again. I told of my meeting to Haimo, who rubbed on the balm — which was indeed healing — and he told me all he had heard. It appeared that those of the family who had been in power were adept at change of position and that without giving offence; at least men were not offended — but what about God? There had been oath-taking and breaking, and the anxiety, yes, the deep pain of followers not able to  take such leaps. I — and indeed Haimo — had been bred to believe in certain secure truths. Must these be questioned? I felt that I had no-one but myself to give the answer, for it appears that the Church also had been two-faced and that was the hardest thing for me to swallow.

What, I thought, would my own Abbot, at home, have said to some of these changes of allegiance? Did he, or did the Church, as a living, most precious whole, approve? And beyond our world was yet another world in which was Rome itself and the great sea between us and Africa and Byzantium and Damascus, many names for cities and powers out of sight, giddying even to name aloud. I wished I was back in innocent childhood before this opening of the world in front of me and yet I had brought it on myself. For the Almighty it might look like ants scurrying from hill to hill over the pine needles in a great forest, unaware of the trees and the sky, but I saw myself as an ant, easily trampled upon. So, where is God's mercy? And how far?

In the days of waiting, which seemed long, we rode down to the sea, a long day's riding through pleasant valleys which had borne good crops of corn and fruit and olive. It was most strange and amazing to see this stretch of water going on and on. I had heard tales and indeed I had made pictures to myself of the sea in which was the great whale that swallowed Jonah, or else the dark sea out of which came the Danes. There had been a picture in one of the books I had seen of the Sea of Galilee and the small boat of the Disciples, so I knew that the sea was blue. Yet it was strange that, as we approached from a hill-top overlooking a small town, this sea appeared to have many colours and waves that seemed made of a kind of lace.

Near a steep path down, we watched what was happening below, while our horses looked for a little grass among the thorny sea-bushes. There were small boats moving on the water, and we could see the line of their nets as if painted behind them. There were also two trading ships, broader than the Danish boats I had seen and hated on the Seine. These had masts and sails. But we did not care to go too near. As it was we were observed, and small traders came climbing up the cliff path with goods, hoping we would buy, and some of the women displaying themselves as offerings. But I turned sharply, for I felt that I had by now been a little cleansed and should forbid myself even a nibble of sin.

Some days later I was bidden to come to another audience with the Lady Dhuoda. I saw that she had been dictating to her special scribe, a young monk. Certainly she could and did put words herself into writing, yet she preferred perhaps to do this act of creation at arm's length. I understood that her intention in these writings was to adorn the idea of faithfulness and obedience from the young toward their elders, and I asked myself whether she might not have in her mind a picture of her father-in-law, now nearly a saint, and hoping that her own sons would sufficiently honour and follow in his footsteps.

I was in some uncertainty over Bernard her husband, at the court of King Charles at Aachen; what could his faith amount to? He had been allied with Pippin — who called himself King of Septimania, and as grandson of the Great Charles could doubtless put forward a noble claim — so who, in these times, can take an oath to whom? How easily can we close our eyes?

With these thoughts I went again to the great hall with the three tables: only one of them was partly set for whoever might come, either for justice or instruction, or even perhaps for neighbourliness and compassion towards a mother whose sons had been snatched from her. There was the sweet smell of new-baked bread and also of a spice which I could not name. Here the wall hangings, some old, some new, took one's mind away into imaginings; they had more figures and flowers in them than those in the hall of the Count of Paris, which I had once admired but now scorned.

In the Lady Dhuoda's own room, which was plainly furnished, more like an abbot's room, I was most struck by the strong smell of roses, even so late in the year; some had been kept back by shading with screens, and some were fallen, sun-dried petals. How, I wondered would heaven smell? Or else the coals of hell?

The Lady greeted me and I saw she had a letter on the small desk beside her, the right height for a woman. On her finger was the same ring but she had no jewels beyond that. I had been told that sometimes she was hard put to it to find money for those who came with some complaint or claim. Even her young son, it was said, had been sent to live with King Charles, more as hostage than guest.

So I came to her with as much courtesy as I could and waited for her to speak. She lifted and held the letter in her hands and smiled. "Imagine," she said, "three young maids in a garden with apple blossom and many small flowers, waiting to be picked for the prettiest chains and bracelets. And what gossip! Not harsh, but laughing and tender. Two with golden hair and one dark. Yes, night-dark, but shining like waves in a deep, dark pool. Each girl has a different common speech, but together all have the noble speech and all can make poems and riddles and knot the words of Latin together as though they were flowers or jewels."

I remember, or almost remember, her very words because she spoke slowly and with such depth of feeling, not so much to me as past me. She would see, I am sure, that I was listening and accepting. But then she turned and looked me straight in the face and spoke in a different voice. "The dark one had come with her father, the Ambassador, and was more precious to him even than his beautiful horses, since he could not bear to leave her with anyone. Yet the time came when he had to take her back across the March, far off. We cried on one another's necks."

She turned to me and her voice became harder. "She went back to the marriage which was waiting for her. And the other fair-haired lass. She is today, I believe, in Aachen, with her brood, fortunate in that." And I saw a sudden tear in her eye. She went on, "But we write, each to the others. And we hope some day to be together again. Even if that can only be possible in heaven, yet so we hope... And the letters pass, yes, even across the mens' battles."

I stayed quiet as a mouse, for she seemed to be smiling as though speaking to a loved one. For a short time she appeared to be looking, not at me but through me, and then, still smiling, she put out her hand with a sealed letter.

I thought to myself, This is my destiny. For good or ill, God help me.

She said, "This letter is for the dark one, the true

beauty of us three. Now look carefully to where it is going and to whom." She added, "It is woman's gossip, most of it. Or so a man would say. But it comes from the heart." I could see her blue eyes filling with tears and suddenly she looked older.

I took the letter in my hand and looked quickly. I read the word Cordoba and asked in a half-whisper, "In the Saracen land?"

"Their greatest city," she said, "and she is married to their greatest man."

I thought, this is beyond me. It is impossible. I cannot. But my hand was gripping the letter. She went on, "You will bring me back the answer. If all is well with her. And then God will smile on you again — as He once did before."

I put the letter under my tunic and shirt, next to my heart and suddenly she said in a different voice, "Brother Milo will give you all you will need for the journey; he will tell you the necessary words, which you must learn by heart, as well as some directions for the road.

"There is one thing I will tell you now. In Cordoba there is a great and beautiful building, call it cathedral if you will. It is larger and more beautiful than any other, even in Rome or Byzantium and the whole Christian world. But also it is a mosque, indeed it was built only as a mosque, for it was built entirely by the Saracens. It is a sacred place for the Moslem Arabs, who must be respected, and beyond that again it is a synagogue and you will also respect the Jews at their prayer. Yes, all can — and do — worship there..."

I had no answer, it was all too difficult, beyond

128

any thoughts I could have. She went on, "It has room for all. Go there. Pray for us all in Frankland and most heartily for our rulers."

I must have murmured something, an acceptance. Suddenly she reached out her hand, saying, "Kiss my hand. And then kiss hers. So that it passes. You will bring me back the answer to my letter, if all goes well. Then God may smile on you again."

I felt that somehow she knew that, and this which I was set to do would be the turning point. I felt the sharp parchment corners of the letter and the little lump of whatever was enclosed within it against my fingers; the curtains were drawn back and I seemed to know what was laid on me to do and be.

SO NOW I went, although in a kind of daze, to Brother Milo, who was seemingly aware of the errand on which I was sent, but shook his head a little sadly. "Yes," he said, "You must go, but it will be well for you to learn a few words of Arabic."

"The Pagan language?" I said, with no wish to soil my tongue with such things.

He shook his head, "No, no! It is a form of noble language, since it reaches out to astronomy and also to mathematics. Indeed it is possible that we have allowed ourselves to be somewhat chained by Roman figuring, which is noble but going the long way round certain philosophical problems." He gave a little cough, as I remember, but later I understood his meaning, when I saw how quickly the folk who used the eastern figuring could come to their conclusions.

He gave me the choice of passing through the March lands or going in a ship to Barcelona. But I was anxious about the horses and how they would fare on the ocean, let alone ourselves. Indeed there were sudden wintry winds coming which might well toss even a large boat.

With his advice I decided to leave the pack horses with our lad who would look after them. I would ride Suelde and Haimo his horse, at first carrying our baggage behind us until we were into the March lands. Once there, we should buy a pack mule, which was the recognised habit on the far side of the mountains. Thus we would look like common travellers and less likely to be robbed.

I settled for a few weeks of learning the language and passing over what I had learned to Haimo, who had also found a young monk who knew many useful words.

My teacher, Brother Adhelm, was an oldish monk who had engaged himself to write a history of the world, that is to say of the world as we know it, leaving out those totally far-off lands, too hot or too cold, whose inhabitants were certainly lost souls, especially those who had been described by Herodotus and Aristotle, who were perhaps half-animals. There had perhaps been a time when the Moslems were beyond that border, but that was long ago.

This monk had, as a young man, travelled not only to Byzantium, of which he often spoke, but to Jerusalem and beyond to the land of the Napateans, who indeed I myself had never even heard of, but this monk said they were great builders and carvers and made little ditches to take spring water far out to their farms and orchards.

For some of his information for this history, Brother Adhelm had to consult books in the Arabic script, which to me was no more easy to read than a spider's web, but he put his finger on a word, spoke it and had me speaking after him. After a while it began to seem no more difficult than Latin had been when I began on it, and the grammar at last began to be apparent. I also learned the modes of addressing that would not offend even the greatest. I keep these sealed even now in memory, although I am never likely to use them again.

By now it was late in the year, though not as near winter weather as it would have been at home. There were sudden cold winds and I had no wish to delay. I remember that I was sure to my bones that we would have trouble, that we might meet with robbers or with parties of young men out for mischief, as I had been myself once. Both Brother Milo and his colleague Brother Adhelm, with whom I spent so many hard hours of learning, had told me that Spain under the Saracen rule was perhaps the safest place in the world, safer than Frankland or, for that matter, Italy. Travellers were respected, whether Moslem, Christian or Jew. All were termed by the rulers *People of the Book*. This was known even to the ploughmen, even to beggars in the street, so I was told.

Yet there was, they said, indeed one small problem. For, on crossing the March and arriving at the far side of these fearsome mountains that bounded Septimania on the south, we would come, not into Spain itself, but into a different kingdom which is neither Frankland nor under the government of the Caliphs. The people of this kingdom speak a different language; they say they have been there forever, though Brother Milo shook his head at this, only adding that they were proud and took offence easily, so caution is needful. But at least most of them would speak and understand the noble tongue.

So, with all this great bagful of cautions and learnings in my head (which I passed on to Haimo) we set off, leaving the vineyards and fields where the corn had long been cut and taken in, and came to the foot of the mountains, where I thought it safest to join with some respectable merchants. We went by hill paths such as I had never seen before; there were many beasts about, among them large bears, which we could sometimes hear and even smell though they did not attack us. For a few days it was hard to see what was ahead, there were so many peaks and valleys and rocks, but at last we came to the March and a company of armed men with fierce looks. It was not so great a trouble as I had feared, for it was true that the noble language was spoken by those in authority, and all knew the Lady Dhuoda and the Lord Bernard. We turned down towards the sea and the great city of Barcelona.

Here I saw my first Saracen men and boys. But I did not yet feel able to use the new words which I had been taught and Latin converse was still everywhere and we ourselves stayed in a small monastery. Both of us had the feeling of being strangers, so we did not stray about the streets looking for noble houses, markets, churches or other memorials.

I was told that there had been hard fighting here against the Saracen invaders and the cathedral had been burnt to the ground. Yet that was past and the town thriving again with a constant coming and going of ships and goods. We did not even go down to the harbour, for I was feeling only that we were in a strange place and must press on. I slept always with the letter under my shirt.

I had been given by Brother Adhelm certain words or strings of words, to say, which indeed were of great use and comfort. Soon enough I had to make attempts at using them and I was happy to see myself understood, even though there might be a little laughter. The inns were clean and our horses well treated, as also was the mule which we had bought with his bridle and rope. Most of the time we travelled near the sea coast; the hills, we were told, often enough harboured wild folk, ready to kill or even eat the wandering stranger, yet perhaps all this was to make us keep to the road and the bridges and great gates where we had a toll to pay. I had learned from Brother Milo how to handle the Spanish coins which he had given me.

Almost always we would join in with other travellers, often for several stages of the way, so that we would get to know one another and I could practice my greetings and small talk. This was for safety's sake, as, in spite of the rule of law which the

Moslems had tried to enforce and which made honest folk safer, there were still brigands around. Indeed we had one such attack in a place where the road left the coast and climbed into the hills. But we beat the brigands back, some of them trailing blood from wounds we had given, and there were compliments both to myself and to Haimo, for the courage and sword skill we had shown. Yet I was somewhat abashed at the pleasure I had found in fighting again in good earnest.

A town or even a big village would always have a safe place for travellers, with a middle space for horses, mules and sometimes cattle or handsome sheep, but never pigs. Around this would be small shelters or huts where one could sleep behind a barred door, though often somewhat plagued by biting fleas or worse. We also came across small monasteries and were gladdened to hear the chanting of psalms or the holy mutter of prayers, where all spoke the noble tongue, though some Latin words were a little twisted. It seemed that the Moslems let them be, so long as they behaved with courtesy and in no way suborned their Moslem lords. In one such place one of the older monks would even have me believe that the Moslems were often near to being Christians. But this I could not countenance. True, they knew and practised certain virtues, but that would not avail them at the Last Judgement. And in a way I was sorry.

Sometimes on that long ride I was almost happy. I seemed to have shed my dark shadow of sin. There was so much to see of differences, of trees and crops and even the wild animals, for example the deer. There was also the strange clothing, both of men and women. Some of the women had their veils pulled across their faces and even the small girls wore veils, nor was it a sign of marriage as with us. They seemed to wear these veils even within the house, where my sisters would have worn their hair loose and wavy. But it was the men's garments that were strangest, for most of them wore long shirts coming down over their knees, and also cloths over their heads, kept in place with a woven tie, sometimes ornamented. It sometimes happened that we would see a troupe of armed men, and leading them perhaps a great man, as it were a lord or count, and they would all be wearing rich and elegant war gear even on such a peaceful errand. Sometimes they would play games with their spears or their bright swords, tossing them in the air and catching them, or riding at some marker in the ground. Haimo and I would stop and watch them, joining in the cheerful din. Their horses were not only beautiful and lively in themselves, but set off by decorated harness — even the baggage mules. And the leaders shone with gold and precious stones on belt and head-gear, as also on the stirrups which were commonly used here, and made it the easier when they spurred their horses into caprioling, as they often did, to the applause of their men.

One such man took an interest in me, whom he spied as a foreigner, but neither merchant nor beggar. We talked — he even had some Latin — and he showed me his sword, which was indeed beautiful, with a curved blade, the edge as sharp as a barber's razor. It was made in Toledo, as I had heard tell. As we spoke in this friendly way, I kept thinking that here was a man whom I must judge as amiable and, I thought, in his behaviour noble, and yet he was most surely destined for hell. I had a strong wish to speak to him of the Lord Jesus and lead him to true belief, and yet I knew that not only would this be a vain endeavour, but also it would be against the other rule which I had always honoured, the rule of courtesy.

I talked much with Haimo on this journey, counting on him always as my half-brother and with more sense than I had over many things. But there was one slip. We were at one of these travellers' resting places, where, as usual, small vendors kept coming to tempt us with their wares, cooked food and drink as well as ropes, buckles, small trinkets and whatever else they might tempt us into buying, including their own favours. Mostly we turned our backs and indeed we were tired enough after a long day in the saddle, and sometimes I would say over parts of the scripture which I knew by heart and which Haimo could join in: they were always a comfort to me.

This night, after our meal, Haimo had said he would be away a little while seeing to the horses. But the day darkened, the noise of the other travellers died down, and I became anxious over what might have happened to Haimo, who was less accustomed to the language than myself and might have been in trouble. As time passed on towards midnight and Haimo not returned I began to be truly anxious. I went over to the horses and I remember that I suddenly found myself in tears and resting my face against Suelde's neck as she turned her head towards me. I came back to our little habitation and waited with increasing fear. At last Haimo staggered in, and it was clear he had been drinking. And more.

I was angry enough, but also anxious, as, although he would drink in measure and often start singing songs which were too full of mockery and bad behaviour for my taste, yet had catchy tunes, he had never before been like this. He started laughing about a girl whom he had been with, using words which were more than dirty. I tried to stop him, using harsh speech, as his master, which truly I did not care to do. But that was not all, for, in a while, there came a girl edging into our little dwelling with long, scented hair and her breasts half showing. I tried to speak sharply but not unkindly, telling her to go, but she clawed at me with warm hands and wet mouth.

"That's the one!" said Haimo, "and I can tell you—"

But I stopped him sharply and pushed out the girl, though she clutched onto me like a briar bush.

I bolted the door against her, though Haimo tried to stop me, speaking about the delights he had got from this girl who was shrieking and whining and demanding money, for it seemed that Haimo had told her that I would pay for all. The worst was that, for a moment I felt a strong temptation for something I had kept at bay since that terrible day when I had seen myself in deep sin. My body longed towards this girl and her scent and softness until, painfully, I had snatched myself away and was down on my knees, with the cold, hard stone of repentance chilling my hot desire. Haimo tried to pull me to my feet and the girl at the far side of the door began to sob as though I had hurt her, as indeed perhaps I had.

I hit Haimo, my own half-brother, across the face and I shouted at the girl to go away, using what I knew was hard abuse in her own language. Haimo, drunk as he was, knew better than to hit me back. He turned away and slumped onto the baggage and in a minute or two was snoring. But I myself was torn with temptation and carnal longing which I had hoped had left me; it was hours before I could sleep. Indeed it was Haimo who woke first and then knelt beside me, asking for pardon, calling me lord and master. But I knew in my soul that I was no better than he and that my feet were still fast in the mud of hell. All that day we rode as it were in a nightmare, neither of us speaking to the other.

CHAPTER FIVE

IT IS HARD

for me, today, to put together all my thoughts and picturing about Cordoba. I dream of that city often enough and most of all the straight, high walls of the castle, which was also a palace,

though there were numerous other, gentler palace buildings. I was never again to see anything approaching what those Caliphs achieved. Yet perhaps I think most of all of the great mosque which Lady Dhuoda had called the cathedral. True enough, as she had said, it was shared between them and ourselves, and also the Jews, with some of whom I became acquainted and found them to be no worse than many a Christian. It was an amazing dream of a building — arches over arches and a great tangle of marble patterns which yet had a precise blend and meaning. The Saracens do not make pictures or statues, but instead pray towards Mecca which must indeed be a great and wonderful town, and of which they speak in parables, for to them it is a kind of Jerusalem.

I found myself forever making comparisons and setting myself questions to which I did not know the answers. Since I now lodged among a Christian community, I must needs listen to them first, but I was careful not to make commitments, since I felt that, if I was to succeed in my task of delivering the letter, I must not appear to the castle or the palace as unfriendly. Above all, I had to learn something of the Saracen nobility, whom I must somehow come not only to speak with, but be allowed some measure of trust. And all this among such a multitude of riches as I had never even dreamed of.

As I understood, there was a great monarch or Caliph far off in the east, in or near to that Jerusalem that they called Mecca and which all of their faith hoped to visit at some time in their lives. But here the Caliph and ruler is called Abd al-Rahman, as indeed so were his father and grandfather called; he is more powerful than many a king, and far richer than any of them. It seemed that, all the same, he was no tyrant and when he gave audience it was said that he would listen to even the lowliest of his subjects, whatever their race or beliefs. I had seen him riding past in the streets of Cordoba which were wide and well-swept daily and always filled with great numbers of folk, buying and selling or simply going about their peaceable way. Haimo and I were staring about us, hearing shouts of praise and pleasure and here, suddenly, was their ruler. I saw at once that the white mare he was riding was as near perfect as one could imagine and also that the turban twisted over his head was hooked with a huge gold-set ruby with another such at his throat. The white mare stepped high and proudly, as though she had a true appreciation, not only of her rider but of the rubies on her own head-band. The men who followed him and whose names the crowd whispered, were scarcely less splendid and the crowd named them with praises which were perhaps truly felt.

Certainly the Caliph Abd al-Rahman was well considered by all the citizens of Cordoba. It was not only that he was just and generous in his dealings, but he appeared to give them much pleasure of the kind they wanted: such as fire-works, new to me and most edifying since they seemed to reach into the heavens among the stars, or else decorated waggons going through the streets with boys dressed as animals giving out cakes. Some of the Christians complained that neither wine nor beer were handed out, since this is forbidden by the sacred book of the Moslem religion. But I, thinking of Haimo, said they had better sense than ourselves over some things. There were also many bonfires lighted in the squares, welcome enough, for now it was winter with sharp cold winds, though only a scatter of snow, rather than our heavy falls at home.

After a few weeks, during which I was wondering what approach to make and feeling the letter sometimes almost burning me, for I kept it always under my shirt, I became aware that some of the Christian community were hatching a plot, which might be only in words as yet, but words can be as dangerous as mad dogs. They believed or pretended to believe that the Lord Himself, and Jesus Christ, was on their side and would work miracles for them. Did they truly believe that, or was it not all a tangle of greed and jealousy?

I could not but know that Cordoba was the finest city I could ever hope to see, with all its beautiful palaces and great houses, all with gardens and, when one could snatch a glance behind the gate, a pool of clear water. Indeed there was clean water to be had in most places; in my travels I had found that Moslem men and boys kept themselves singularly clean, washing from head to foot even in winter. There were always bands of slaves sweeping pavements as if they were cloisters, but these had shops on the inner side where all kinds of craftsmen practised their skills on metals, both base and precious, or on sweet-smelling wood or woven hangings or boots of fine leather, and the most splendid carpets I had ever seen on which one would be happy to sleep and find good dreams: in short, every kind of merchandise and luxury, making nonsense of all such things I had ever seen before.

And yet they were mostly heathens. Or were they? I felt myself pulled this way and that. These Saracen Moslems, as I was told and indeed could see from what was going on around me, considered that not only Christians, but the Jews also, were in some way worshipping the same God and had the same kind of laws and hopes, indeed might go to the same heaven. So that we were all in a kind of brotherhood. But yet, I said to myself, is this not too easy a way? Is Satan perhaps at my heels?

Whether this was so or not, I knew in my bones that I neither liked nor trusted a certain man called Alvaro, who was deeply engaged in plots against the rule of the Caliph. He would half confide in me, then turn away, keeping the yolk of his. plot hidden. This became painful and disturbing, since if I went to the great church or mosque, it seemed that all were in one bond. Here surely, for all of us in the congregation it was the same. Here was the worship of God, the trust in God's will and surely it must be the same God, since all acknowledged that there is no other God. And if there were different patterns of worship? All could rise into eternity.

I had also watched the Jews at their worship. Many of what I took to be their saints were the same as ours, such as Abraham. Were they conspiring? I did not think so.

I dared not say this aloud, even to Haimo, though I think he guessed how I was thinking; still less could I speak of this to Father Eulogia, who might feel some approval for the conspiracies which were hatching.

Whenever I was in a suitable company, therefore, I would lead onto certain questions, testing the gossip and finding out answers that I had to know. For all the time my problem was how to deliver the letter. I knew that the lady to whom it was addressed was a wife of Abd al-Rahman, one of his chief wives, for the custom is to have more wives than one, up to four. A rich man would also have other women, not secretly but as custom and accepted manners. The ladies who were married to the Caliph lived apart, having separate apartments in the great palace, which also, I was told, had fruit trees and flowering trees and fountains of pure water.

I told nobody that I had a letter, but only mentioned the name of the lady as someone I had heard tell about. It was said that she was beautiful and generous, but they might have said that of an old witch if she had been married to the Caliph.

So I became most anxious to find some other place to live and to leave this man Alvaro and his stories which were far from the truth. It became clear that his plots might even hatch, for now he spoke of the suborning of poorer men such as gate keepers, suggesting that I should be the one to approach them. I must certainly break with him. But how? Where should I go?

I talked it well over one night with Haimo and it was he, fully as anxious as I was, who put it to me that we might shelter under the wing of Count Gomez, who was a church-goer and known to be well thought of by the Bishop; he was also received by the Caliph and had some kind of authority in the city.

I sought an audience with him and he, it appeared, had noticed my presence in the city, or had it pointed out to him. He was indeed a courteous and hospitable man and when I said that I was glad to have shaken off my first hosts, he smiled and said I was well out of that barnyard. "One day the farmer comes out of his door and wrings certain necks," he said.

Yet I did not at first know how fortunate I had been to be accepted into the household of Count Gomez.

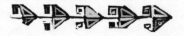

CHAPTER SIX

IN AVOIDING the plots and machinations

of Alvaro and his friends and indeed of Father Eulogia, who could always call up texts which would further the designs of this group of rebellious

Christians, was I not in some way denying my Christian loyalties? Was I being tested, and failing? Or was I caught by my promises, my oath to the Lady Dhuoda, which could be drawing me away from my surely more deep and powerful Christian loyalty? If, as I had thought so painfully on the long

Autumn journey, I was a damned soul because of what I had done in the forest and the innocent blood crying at me, was I yet further endangering myself by a kind of admiration of the Moslem rule, allowing myself to condone their heathen scriptures and rule? I tried to find some saying in my psalter or in the Scriptures themselves which would give me guidance. But in the end I had to come to my own decisions.

Alvaro was angry when I told him that I had been invited elsewhere and spoke of better stabling for Suelde as part of my reason, which was true enough, but not my main intention. I added that nothing he had said, perhaps not meaningfully or in jest, would be passed on, although I had already spoken of it to Count Gomez. But indeed I thought that most of his talk was a nonsense, and had little of true commitment to the Christian church behind it.

I was more than glad when Haimo and I took ourselves, our horses and our pack-mule, off to the house of Count Gomez, and established ourselves in a small way. The chapel which Count Gomez had built and decorated was, so to say, part of the house and I spent some nights there in the cold and dark, asking forgiveness of all my sins, past and present, great and small. It seemed that stories of this went round the ears of some in the house and perhaps made Count Gomez more friendly towards me.

He showed me his library which had a marvellous bounty of books, some in the Arabic script but mostly in Latin. There was not merely history, including the lives of many saints, some new to me, but many works on the courses of the stars, the various uses of herbs and roots, as well as others on navigation and directions of storms, and indeed the products of a great quantity of thinking and questioning.

There was an elderly and, I think, truly wise monk

147

who had charge of the library. His name was Father Beringuer and he was from a noble family. We had much talk together and I told him of my promise to Lady Dhuoda, even showing him the sealed letter, which I had always kept safe under my shirt. I remember well that he took the package in his hands and sniffed at it, giving me a sideways look. I blurted out that I changed my shirt almost every week, to which he answered "But how often do you wash your body?"

Now it came to me that this might be something I should see to, and yet, until then I had never thought about it, simply having done what others in my station of life had thought fit. The long and short of this was that Father Beringuer took me, in a most fatherly way, to one of the great public baths, of which there were three or four in Cordoba, where I had myself cleaned, in hot water and cold, with scrubbing and sea sponging from head to feet.

It became clear to me that most of the people of Cordoba washed themselves totally clean at the least once a week. This had been brought in by the Saracens, who loved water, perhaps because they came from lands where it was scarce and precious. These public baths cost little unless one had a mind to be rubbed or oiled after the cleansing, so I sent Haimo to be washed, since, once I had started I began to understand that most unwashed persons stank. I heard also from Father Beringuer that the hardest thing in being a monk was not, as I had supposed, the vow of chastity, but the ban on public bathing, most especially in summer.

So there I was, washed, and in a while this same Father Beringuer said to me that the wife of the

Count, the Lady Elvira, had invited me to an audience and also that she had been told about the letter. I was more than happy to hear that and the Father accompanied me to another part of Count Gomez' great house. We passed through arches and beside a square pool with a design of white marble and a fountain constantly filling it, the water perhaps slipping away to yet another pool, for there were many of these, and the pleasant sound of water throughout the house.

We came onto a terrace that looked out over a small garden which even now had a few flowers of some kind that I did not know and the Lady Elvira was there, sitting on cushions of shining silk and sipping a kind of sweet drink that was much liked by the Spanish people, and beside her was another woman, veiled so that only her eyes showed, dark and large, for the custom was to ring the eye itself with a kind of paste or powder.

This other it seemed, was the second wife of Count Gomez. But was it possible that she was the one to whom I must give the letter and whose hand I was to kiss, as from her old play-mate? Surely not. I had been told that the lady I sought was married to the Caliph himself. This one might at best be a go-between. I could not begin to know whether or not she approved of my manners or appearance. The eyes alone said nothing.

The Lady Elvira questioned me closely and I felt a little as though I was still being schooled. Where was I from? Who were my parents, and after that, my grand-parents on both sides? Were they related to so-and-so, or, in particular this or that uncle? I was scolded because I could not be totally certain about some of them, more especially my grandmother's father — or was it uncle — who had held some kind of important office at the Court of the great Charles. But I had forgotten what exactly it was.

"These things should be written down," said the Lady Elvira, "and you are a bad child to pay so little heed to your forbears, who, under God, made you."

I could only say that I was sorry and would take care, if, God willing, I was to see my parents again, to write all this down with pen and ink.

Why was I here, in Cordoba? Cautiously I said that I had a letter to deliver, written by the Lady Dhuoda, wife of Bernard of Septimania.

"That wretch!" was the comment, and I could not but agree, knowing what I did.

"How does she do?" asked Lady Elvira, tapping with her fingers, as she watched me. I answered that she was writing a book for her young son's edification. "He will need it," was the answer, "if he takes at all after his father."

"Yet his grandfather was a truly good man," I began cautiously.

She laughed. "The lad was begotten before his dad turned into a saint. And I can tell you, today's Bernard is as little like a saint as can come."

I was a little perturbed at that. "So what has today's Bernard done that is so wrong?" I asked, still kneeling before Lady Elvira.

She threw a cushion down for me to sit on. "He has slipped from one King to another and back again and has found ladies in both courts who pleased him more than his wife. He broke all his marriage promises to her, just as he broke all his oaths, both to

150

Pippin and Charles — and maybe Lothar!"

I had no answer. What she said was terrible, but it answered a question. I said, "I know that the Lady Dhuoda is much esteemed by all her household and indeed all her neighbourhood. Perhaps too much is laid upon her, and little thanks. Except that it is well to be loved by those around."

"And well she might be loved!" said Lady Elvira. "And now this letter which you are carrying — to whom is it addressed?"

"To her old play-mate, from long ago in Aachen, the Lady Aisha."

"Ah, that was well. Yes, it will bring happiness. So, young man, you hope to deliver it to that same lady?"

I assented.

She smiled a little, then turned to the other lady. "Have you not guessed yet?" she said. "This is Aisha's sister!"

I felt even a little angry, because they had been teasing me. But I swallowed my anger quickly, thinking that teasing mostly means liking, and soon we were all laughing. After this they talked to one another or gabbled, for both were in giggles of laughing now and all was in a mixture of Latin and this Arabic that was also the language of Cordoba.

I myself had begun to listen to a sound of horse hoofs, at the gallop, and cries and shouts — certainly not war cries, but great excitement and sometimes a clapping of hands. The conversation of the two ladies broke off. They were on their feet and I, of course, jumped up at the same time.

"Come!" said Lady Elvira, and, over her shoulder,

"and bring the cushions!"

For they were hurrying along the terrace to a small gate, leading to yet another terrace, with an awning and a small rail between it and a wide piece of flattened ground, where half a dozen young boys were riding and hitting a ball about. Lady Elvira clapped her hands and shouted. One of the boys trotted up, dropped on one knee and grinned up at her. "My son," she said.

Another boy was off his horse and an elderly man, well dressed, caught him and gave him a cut across the buttocks with a cane switch. The boy ran back from where we were, rubbing his behind and grimacing.

"That one," said Lady Elvira, "is Aisha's boy — you must tell Dhuoda. He had pulled his horse and missed the ball. But he will learn. Now you must watch. This is a different game."

They were all gathered at the far end of the field, with their horses, and the men had prepared a course. Down came the boys at a gallop, with light spears, for hunting rather than war, and tried to pick up the rings which had been lain ready on the ground. Half of them missed, but Aisha's son, whom I watched with the greatest interest, was now the best of them. Yet, as I could see, much depended on their horses, who knew the game even better than their riders.

I found myself choosing in my mind which of these horses I would have if they were mine to choose from. I could see them swishing their tails with pleasure if their riders did well. Such beautiful horses. I wondered whether, if it could be arranged for Suelde to bear a foal by one of these. If, just before I left — if all went well... But much might happen yet.

We watched the games for a while. I kept thinking of the Lady Dhuoda and what I could tell her about her friend's boy, a handsome lad, perhaps a little younger than her William, with skin of a delicate brown, which I was becoming to admire more than sun-chapped pale skins. The Caliph's son: what would his future be? Could he stand up to the many temptations which would be showered on him? To do this without the help of our Lord God, to whom we can turn! Yet it seems that their prophet had left a great writing with rules of conduct which if they were followed, and the reader truly understood them... But was it not hard enough to be a Christian and to follow what one knew for certain was the right way?

Now Lady Elvira jogged me on the arm. "Are you dreaming?" she asked. "Is this too like heaven? Or some other Paradise? For there are more than one." And she laughed. "Now," she said, "we will arrange the next meeting. Meanwhile I shall take you to the stables, for I could see where your eyes were. But you must not forget that your own mare is a good beast to have taken you safely so far from home... Never forget her for others."

"Yes," I said. "I think I understand. We must always be true to those we have loved." And suddenly I thought of the Saxon Wolfin, whom too I had loved.

I waited, yes, but with a strong conviction that all would be well. Count Gomez and the Lady Elvira asked me often to their table and had me tell about my own life, and especially about the Count of Paris and our oath-taking, and the dealings which the Count may have made with King Charles. I remember Count Gomez raising his eyebrows a little, since he had heard certain tales which were best not passed on, for it might stretch my loyalty too far. I begged him to tell me, but he smiled and said I would know soon enough. Indeed I did not know for many months, and it was my father who had to bear the burden.

By now, in Cordoba, there were still cold winds, yet the sun had begun to give us a little heat and small flowers crept out. Above all the almond trees were most beautiful, especially when looked at from under the flowers into the deep heavens above. They had been brought to Spain by the Saracens three generations back and were now flourishing. I had never eaten almonds before.

At last one morning, I was waiting at the locked gate of a garden, surrounded inwardly with almond trees, in which I was to find the Lady Aisha, or should I simply say the Queen. Our meeting was already laid out in my imagining, as though it had already come to pass. So now, in my remembrance, I am caught between what I had intended and what truly passed between us. Yet I cannot begin to think of it without also remembering the musician Ziryab.

I had heard singing before in Cordoba. There were street singers, some greatly talented, round whom a crowd might gather, perhaps throwing in money if the singer seemed to tire. Yet for the most part I did not care much for this singing, which seemed to me to be too much a wailing or a shouting. But then I heard Ziryab, the Court singer, and that was different. His voice was, to my ear, something between a man and a woman. I did not enquire why this was, although I fear that I know. They did this thing to promising boys. Yet Ziryab's was also like an angel's voice or so I thought, calling one gently to listen and become one with heaven. At the gate of the Caliph's garden, barred and sentried, with this music floating over me, and knowing that all would be open when the time came, I stood waiting, as I had been told, and, beyond the singing, there was a sweet and cheering scent, I think from some early flowers, larger than our own wild snowdrops and pale gold. The Caliph had brought the roots of many flowers that flourish at the very far side of all lands and seas, in Arabia itself perhaps, and this included roses that were more thickly petalled than any of ours and of diverse colours. I was never fortunate enough to see these roses in bloom, but the Lady Elvira had bowls full of the dried, musky petals, to scent the rooms of the whole house.

The song ended and a very black man, with a great axe at his side, who looked as if he could easily pick up an ox and throw it over his shoulder, came up and opened the gate with a great jarring of iron as the bolt came out of its socket in the ground, and the bars across scraped back. I was beckoned through onto a path between flowers. The singing of Ziryab went on. I carried the letter in my hand and hoped that the flower scent would cling to it.

Then there was bowing and kneeling and the correct courtly words said, while, for a little, the singing was softer. I remember with great precision how she was, the Queen. She was lightly veiled over a soft dark cloud of hair, but not across her face, perhaps because she was more royal than female, yet tight across her neck. I could see that her face was a little lined around the mouth and nose, sending me sharply into remembrance of the Lady Dhuoda. But she, as the fashion was, wore kohl around her eyes which were in some way deeply dark and questioning, so that one must turn away one's own eyes in confusion. She wore many jewels, including a kind of light crown over her veil. I must needs suppose that the Caliph had more riches than almost any man alive. I thought briefly of this as she took the letter into her hands and murmured something which was blurred by the singing of Ziryab behind the trees.

She opened the letter and then she moved her head a little and the singing stopped. She beckoned me forward until I knelt so close that I could watch her lips moving as she read the letter. At last she looked up. As she began to speak I thought how wonderful it was that the noble tongue had spread over the world of the literate and that Latin would last for ever even if Rome itself came into destruction.

The little lump in the letter which I so often had felt against my chest was wrapped in silk which she pulled apart. She saw that it was a ring set with an amethyst. She then read the inscription and smiled to herself and slipped it onto her finger, silver among her gold, but not, I thought, less cherished.

She looked from it to me and raised her head. "Tell me truly," she said, "how it goes with my play-mate."

I could not lie to her. "The Lady Dhuoda," I said, "is dictating a letter, a very noble letter, addressed to her own son William, yet to be read by all the world, since it is in praise of fealty and obedience."

156

"And her husband? You do not speak of him."

I hesitated, uncertain whether I should say what might be unwelcome words. At last I said, "I fear he does not fulfil his duties towards her."

"Ah," she said. "That must be the worst. For any woman. Allah be praised, I do not suffer it."

I remember it shocked me for a moment to hear those words, but then I was glad, yes, truly glad that this great lady whom I saw for the first time, about whom I could know nothing, had this happiness even though it came to me in deeply un-Christian words.

She went on to ask how many children had blessed the Lady Dhuoda and when I said two boys, she frowned a little. "I have been blessed with three boys and two little maidens — see, there is one of them." She pointed, smiling towards a thick bush and a girl-child peeping at us. "She will learn manners by watching," the Queen said, "but I think you have seen my big lad, he and his horse. The one who, if my prayers are answered, will grow to be a strong and virtuous ruler."

I could only murmur an answer, since it seemed I was glimpsing a page of history. Then she asked me again for more about her old playmate with whom she had shared the happiness of youth, which, as I indeed knew painfully, was the only pure happiness there is, so that our dearest wish must always be to become the children of God. She told me she did not wonder that Dhuoda was writing a book, since she had always been the one to write verse and riddles. "But I," said the Queen, "have made a small book of riddles for you to take back to her. And tell me, does she still have that little crooked smile?"

I tried to answer, and again, when she asked, "Does she make daisy chains now?" I said that I had come in the wrong season, but at least I knew she cared much for flowers and herbs. "Ah," said the Queen. "You shall take seeds back to her. Perhaps even a root. A young almond tree." She turned to one of the older women beside her and asked something. Then to me, "What scent does she use now?"

I said that I was sorry I did not know, but I always thought of summer when I was in the room she used. "And you never asked," she said, "Baby!" And she laughed at me.

So it went, and then more questions. Seeing I might be tired kneeling, she threw me a cushion. Again there were more questions. At last I took my courage into my tongue and told her of the kiss that I must pass on, hand to hand, but that I dared not ask.

She went quiet for a short space and I feared that I had offended, but she called beyond me and then came the singer Ziryab with his little lute for accompaniment. He looked older when I saw him close, even with a touch of grey in his hair and his face beardless and somewhat drawn across the cheek bones.

They spoke for a small time and I withdrew a little. But then he began to sing and I could have wept, for it was as though the singing came from inside me, fumbling round my heart. And then the Queen beckoned and held out her hand and I kissed it and inhaled the scent of it and hoped that somehow I could take all this back to the Lady Dhuoda.

Yes, she also gave me royal gifts, both to take back to her dear play-mate and for myself, of which there were two which made me happier than I can say. One was a Toledo blade, a short sword, light but of perfect sharpness so that it could cut right through a hank of wool. And the other was a colt from the royal stables, not truly broken, but clearly of great promise. Yet it was my lips which felt her hand, so that, so long as I live, I can never forget her.

I WAS NOW

eager for return to Frankland but, with all these royal gifts and above all a letter to take back to the Lady Dhuoda, I must travel differently.

I thought to myself that the return letter must again lie next to my heart, but this time on cleaner flesh, for I was now determined to continue, if it was in any way possible, the habit of washing. I said my farewells to Count Gomez and to the Lady Elvira who preened herself on the success of my errand, and also to Father Beringuer, who gave me a strong blessing. I wished now that I had taken more will to read the many books there were in this house, but there was no longer time.

It came about that I was to be accompanied, at least as far as the March, by six well-armed men, four from Count Gomez and two from the palace. I was told exactly what I was to give them at the end and provided with the money which I wore on my belt. It all seemed unneedful to me, but less so when we were attacked by some number of robbers on a twist of the hill road not far from the bounds of the Saracen empire. We beat them off, easily enough once they had a taste of our weapons, but Suelde had a cut on her shoulder, and I a grazed leg, and Haimo, who was holding onto the royal colt which was bursting with excitement and squealing to the skies, had a huge bruise along one thigh, but whether from the colt or from something thrown was not certain. As for me, I had one splendid cut with the new blade, taking off one robber's hand, club and all. It was all over quickly and after that we were mostly on safe roads, joining up with other well-armed folk making the same way.

At the March, where we met the same dark-haired men whom we had seen at our first entry, Count Gomez' guards turned back, but the two from the palace made it known that their orders were to escort the Queen's letter which I held as far as its destination. I was glad enough to accept this, for it was not only the letter, but the other gifts, both to the Lady Dhuoda and myself, which were wrapped in heavy cloth. I wondered a little what the Queen had sent to her playmate, but knew well that it was from the heart.

When we came over and down into Septimania, we were into the bustle of the farm year starting again, ploughs carried out into the fields, oxen harnessed. At last we were in sight of the hill and the gates and strong wall of Uzès, and suddenly I seemed to meet with the self I was when I first came in sight of all this. That self had been in bitter distress and fear of the hell-fire which he could not but expect. But the new self felt that at last he had blessing, he had been cleansed, at least so far as a mortal, sinful man can become clean through God's mercy, channelled through the death of His Son Jesus. And I think, looking at me, Haimo guessed that all was well.

So we came at last, up through the town, which if it seemed little compared with what I had seen in the last months, was yet welcoming, and I dismounted, to be embraced by Father Milo, Brother Adhelm and others of the monks. We rode up to the castle, where the Lady Dhuoda embraced me and there was much cheer and shouting. But I could not at once speak with her, since she must go into the great hall where a table was being set for the Saracen soldiers, while Haimo could stop the servants from pouring them wine or offering them bacon. He and I needed also to stop too close admiration of the colt who by now was docile and gentle with me and Haimo, but was not so with strangers.

When at last I was allowed time with the Lady Dhuoda, she seemed easier in her mind, perhaps because she had ended her book, which was of great complexity, being partly in verse or else some other kind of patterning. This lady understood very well the rhythms of both prose and verse, some of which go back to the ancient Roman poets, although they are also fitted to our own times. There was even a kind of riddling in both the verse and the prose of her book, so that it was to be understood very deeply.

There had been a first copy made into the form of a book small enough to be carried on the body; one of the monks of Gelone, Wislabert, was now on his way with it to the lady's elder son, at the Court of King Charles, the now acknowledged rightful King of the Franks. The boy — for he was only some fifteen years old, was doubtless being watched and judged, lest he make a false step, a hard thing for someone too young to be always watching himself. Surely it is better to be the son of an honest shepherd or wood-cutter than to be the son of a great man who must watch every movement lest he be suspect of some treachery.

However, I was not making judgements, least of all about the family of the Lady Dhuoda whom I held always in great honour and this although it was beyond me to understand how her husband could be so cold to her, even to the point of snatching away her babe from its cradle, where surely, it would be safer than at Court with only nurses. I understood how hurt she had been, but could do little to help her, except to give her the letter. Yet first she asked that the two Saracen soldiers should be acclaimed as friends and should show their gifts, which were certainly beautiful, since they were mostly silks and embroideries of great value, as well as some small plants which had been most carefully bundled, among them roses and many seeds, including those of the pomegranate tree which was not yet known on our side of the March.

Seeing me, she must have guessed that I had

163

brought what she wanted most of all. After she had read it and after the tears which were yet joyful tears, an assurance that a certain thing which had been the best part of her life, was still there, still strong, she turned to me to add every embroidery on the handing over of her letter in Cordoba, to repeat again and again every movement, every smallest thing that still held in my memory. She called me again the next day and twice more, sometimes asking some little thing or obliging me to go over yet again all I had seen, felt, dreamed, above all feared. I must tell her about the music and in what way it differs from the music we know and love. I told her about the kiss, and she took my hand, so that I must needs point to the exact spot and let her, in turn, kiss it.

I knew well that this was what the Queen herself intended. I told her also about the Queen's young son playing the game with his lance, trying to leave in her mind a picture of the beautiful horses and their young riders. So from time to time she wept a little and I found myself longing to give her some comfort, yet not knowing what or how.

In the end I felt empty, there was no more to give. I knew I must escape, go north again to the oak and alder country, even to the lands which the Danes covetted and which we must guard with our own blood. I began also to be aware that, now that I was cleansed and strong again, my first duty was to my home and above all, to my father as his heir. And it came to me sharply that I did not at all know how things had gone, whether there had been troubles or even deaths, so I became truly anxious and had dreams in which were all kinds of disasters falling on my home and my family.

164

Yet, had I stayed only a few weeks longer, I might have been able to give a helping hand to Lady Dhuoda during the shock of her husband's death. For the Count Bernard was accused of treason and all his enemies and such as harboured jealousy and hatred came together against him, and Louis, the King, had him executed.

I do not know whether the boy had been made to see this. Perhaps, for the courts of Kings are places of deep cruelty. If that was done, did the sad young William get any comfort from the little book and the love of his mother so deeply expressed in it? I do not know. These things are hidden from human eyes or knowledge. Yet I do know that many of Count Bernard's riches and estates were taken by his enemies or by the King himself, although not, I believe, the castle of Uzès and the nearer lands.

As for the lady's own sorrow, I can only guess. Even though this man had given her sore usage, yet he was her husband and she must have been left in fear and sadness. I can only hope and believe that the clergy of Gellone, and indeed the spirit of her father-in-law (if indeed he had become a true saint) stood by her, and that the Lord God in heaven dropped down the comfort upon her which mankind had not given, unless in so small a way as I myself had done with the letter I brought from Cordoba.

CHAPTER EIGHT

BEFORE

that direful message and the disasters following it had reached the Lady Dhuoda, I myself was half way to my home, travelling north with the Spring and the early

leaves, away from the grey olives and the hard-clipped vineyards. As my adventures dropped behind me, I found myself again talking more to Haimo, who had never complained or back-questioned me, and indeed to the boy who had cared for our pack horse, which had been well fed and was now more heavily loaded, although Suelde carried my best gifts from the Queen, which I would always take with me under my thick cloak, or wherever we slept. Mostly we joined up with other travellers, heading north, perhaps clerics but also wandering lads who reminded me of my old self, yet more often merchants of one kind or another. I had many offers for the Saracen colt, but I would always shake my head.

Now and then we had news, mostly of fighting or of taunting messages from one powerful man to another, yet more often it was ourselves who gave news to others, often about Spain and the wonders I had seen. Once, stopping at a monastery, I was forced to listen to a sermon about the wickedness of the Saracens and how they would all be roasted in hell-fire, but I found that I could no longer believe this. I knew in my soul otherwise, that in the end they worshipped the same God, only under another name. And what is the worth of a name? I began planning to take up my own Abbot at home in this argument − yet no − for he could never see it my way and indeed I must keep this to myself, or to Haimo, for I think he reads my very thoughts and sometimes takes them for his own.

We went further and further into a countryside I half knew, often stopping at monasteries or Abbeys which gave hospitality to well-spoken travellers. I tried to keep myself well washed and combed but it was not easy. Sometimes they would remember or half remember me, but scratched their heads a little, comparing me then with now. Yet I avoided the houses or castles where the company of boasting and violence, of which I had been one, was still in control.

There had been girls, also, and I did not wish to

167

see them again with their aprons pushing out, whoever the fault might lie with. In this kind of company I was welcomed once or twice with dirty jokes and sometimes some sharp anger which I could well understand. But when we found ourselves near to the forest where I had been truly seized by the devils of hell, Haimo took Suelde by the bridle, saying that we were on the wrong path, so that we made a great circle away from it.

Once or twice on this journey I was almost pulled into quarrels which could have led to blood-shedding. But I mastered my temper, and sometimes Haimo's, if he thought that I had been insulted. I gave alms when I could and even sold a ring I was wearing and which had been given to me by Count Gomez, to help a poor family whose house had been burnt down and cattle slaughtered in a small war.

Once I asked Haimo if he would look for a marriage once we were back, but he only laughed and said he would see what was on offer. I knew there had been a girl in Cordoba that he was loath to leave, yet even when they bedded he knew it could never come to a marriage. Perhaps he lied to her. I did not ask.

There was another talk I had with him in the height of a Spring day so beautiful that one could not but have in mind the Resurrection. I spoke to Haimo with words of this and all at once he said, "So Wolfin will be with us again."

And if Wolfin, I thought — and it was a happy thought that stayed with me — why not the Saracens? That was too deep water, I thrust it aside. Yet such thoughts returned to me. And also to Haimo. But I said to him that we must needs leave such notions to the Church and perhaps what we must think of first was our commitment on earth to our fellow men, and above all the question of loyalty. Yet I could not have supposed that this great question would fall on me as quickly as it did.

One day we were in known country and here and there we would pass people working and singing. But what would I find?

I asked in a small village, speaking my father's name in a light voice. When the answer came, after some scratching of head, at least I knew he was alive. We rode on and first the tower of the Abbey came in sight and then our house with its strong walls, almost a small castle. But I had seen so many. Soon the thatched roof, with the smoke rising out of the great stone chimney, and nearby there was a tall boy and yes, it was my brother Ulric.

So there was much running and shouting and embracing and I was in the hall and it smelled the same. Then came the gifts, a fine square of silk for my mother with embroidery round the edges. It was better than the silk she had been given from the Count of Paris, I had made sure of that. She threw her arms round my neck, whispering that she had been praying every night for my safety. I had also a small kerchief for my young sister. My mother told me that Hiltrud had borne a son, so now I was an uncle.

I cared most for my brother Ulric. He had shot up like a Spring sapling, with a sprinkle on his cheeks that would soon be the beginnings of a man's beard. But I found him in a high mood, and after questioning, found that he was hoping for a fight in which he could use his sword. He had to see my

169

own sword and to run his fingers along it. When I questioned him he said that our father was at the far borders of our lands, looking for a troop of men, for he was in a mood for war. "Now that you are back," said young Ulric, "it will go well. This new sword of yours is truly a killer."

But I was deeply anxious. I felt I had seen and done enough killing for a lifetime. I had also seen the delights and excitements of peace, when a great city, such as Cordoba, stood clean and beautiful and full of objects of interest and astonishment. And besides that there were people with whom even a stranger might have converse on such subjects as astronomy or medicine or arithmetic — for such things can be brought into great argument, to the edification of any person of parts. Beyond that there were the fine materials and objects of beauty to be bought and sold, games and sports to be watched or joined. And if in Cordoba and among the foreign people, why not here in Frankland? For all at once it came to me that we had fooled ourselves for a long time, allowing discontent and jealousies to grow and flourish, fostering quarrels even between close relatives, thinking only of a little booty, a little excitement, a little killing.

So what was my brother Ulric thinking about? What fantasy? And worse, what was in my father's mind and how should I meet him?

It came to me that these thoughts I had been having were truly a matter for the Church, so while I waited for my father's coming — and now I could see that my mother was anxious and a little distressed — I would put them to the test. I went therefore to my Abbot, who had meant so much to me as a boy. As I rode over I was deciding to say little or nothing of my days in Cordoba, since he saw them only as a slip into the sin of acquiescence to a great Satan. And I knew in my bones that this was not the true picture.

Instead, after our greetings, I spoke of the Lady Dhuoda and above all of the Abbot's old friend, Father Milo, whom he had not seen for many years, and who had trusted me with, conjuring me to keep them safe, some little pretty boxes full of the seeds of his own garden herbs which he thought would be new to the north. My Abbot was deeply interested in my views of the Lady, to whom God had given such powers of writing and poetry, but had not spared her over her life as wife and mother. Above all his welcome of me was as warm as I had expected and hoped for.

Then we fell to talk about how things had gone over the months when I had been away from home. He had heard some tales of our first doings which had distressed him greatly, but he could see that I looked back with sorrow on my young self. Indeed, he did not press me to speak of those days which indeed had brought me deep suffering in my repentance and now, I hoped, were long past.

While I was speaking of the Lady Dhuoda and her troubles which had so much to do with her husband, his ambitions and perhaps broken loyalties, my Abbot began to pour out on me his anxieties about my father who had received a message of great alarm. It came from the Abbot Hugh of Saint Quentin who was, as I must know, a son of the Great Charles, though not of any wife: a King must have concubines as King David had in the scriptures.

171

Indeed my Abbot would have gone on sadly and in detail on the habits of Kings, but I said, "Yes, but what was the message?"

"To join him," said the Abbot, "in a strong intention to make himself the King of Frankland, at least of the western half."

"Against King Charles?" I asked sharply.

"Yes. Since Charles is young — perhaps too young for so great a station — and Abbot Hugh who was tonsured as a boy in order to keep him from rivalry with good King Louis, is of the older generation, nearer to the Great Charles— "

But I took him up sharply, "My father and I — with your support, Father — took the oath to Charles, through the Count of Paris."

"It is this same Count who is behind this," said my Abbot, "though I do not much care for him, but he believes the true leader is Abbot Hugh who is well known and respected everywhere for the strength of his heart and his compassion -"

I said, "There is no compassion in war. Only anger and hurting."

My Abbot turned half away and said, "It is for your noble father to decide. Perhaps tomorrow we shall see him again, and if he has called up his men— "

But I took my leave sharply, swung into the saddle and left with the total intention of showing this father of mine, on his return, the wrong and folly of what he was intending and the oath-breaking it would mean.

That evening I stayed mostly with my mother, who seemed to cling to me. We sat in the small room above the hall, where she had her spinning and weaving. There was also a pleasant smell of herbs. It was here that she told me, with a little weeping, how she had borne another little son, but before time and he had died, the cross sprinkled over him while his body still moved but his small eyes were shut in death.

"He had eyes like yours" she said, "and I was in much pain. But your Lord Father— "

She paused, looking over into the corner, with her own eyes swimming. And then: "But men, it seems, have to be that way, taking what their bodies crave and not caring— "

She gave a little choking cry and I took her in my arms and felt her tears warm on my face.

I thought to myself, When I marry, I shall honour my wife, whoever she is, and never give her cause for such tears.

Yet I also knew that my father was better than many a man. I thought of the Lady Dhuoda and then, all at once, of Queen Aisha.

Very soon I would have to speak to Haimo and to my brother Ulric, and also, I thought, to some of the men who were well thought of and likely to agree with my own judgements: this meant, for a start, Walakind and some of his family and comrades. They had understood that in the journey to Paris and the oath-taking there had been, not any pledge to the Count of Paris, but beyond him, to the King, that is, to Charles. It was not hard to understand therefore that if the Count broke his own oaths to the King, we had no obligation to follow. Indeed, if we did, and if things went badly with this adventure, we would be in very great trouble. All we had might be forfeited.

I said to them that such changes were likely to fail, but more importantly, we in Frankland had had enough of these small wars, these jealousies and betrayals which were tearing us to pieces, setting brother against brother, uncle against nephew.

"A few may gain but many must lose. All will end in death and pain, killing of beasts, ruining of crops, burning of houses, raping of women, blood, blood! Do you trust my judgment?" I asked.

Walakind said, "Yes," very soberly.

Others followed, and so we waited.

Haimo kissed me and said, "I am yours."

I felt my cheek against his neck and the pulsing of blood and I whispered, "Yes, I know."

Even better, Ulric suddenly said he was proud of me, he would follow me even against our father. Yet somehow I guessed that he had a half-thought that it might end in some kind of real fighting between our father and me and I knew that this would be the wrong way. I must somehow make my father recognise that he must keep his deeper oath to King Charles, even though it meant that the lesser one which he had taken to the Count of Paris must be broken.

The night went by. Strangely I had a deep sleep with none of the nightmares which had so often persecuted me.

Then came my father and a mob of armed men from the furthest parts of our lands. He had ridden most of the night and was tired and somewhat aching, as I could see, and only wanting sleep, as I could see but did not allow, for he was bound to welcome me back, his eldest son and heir. He was happy at first but then became hurt and angry when he saw, quickly enough, that I was cutting across his intentions and also across some vain expectations he had made up of what good things might come out of this fighting.

We talked, both sitting on our horses, his larger than mine but drooping with tiredness. As I remember it now it was like a game and I won it. Yet it was more than a game, for it was about the meaning of an oath, which is perhaps also the meaning of our promises to God, since there is an oath between God and mankind. And suddenly my father was swaying in his saddle with tiredness, and went in. But he left his men standing and Walakind and others were speaking to them and they began to understand and some came to kiss my hand and swear fealty to me.

Late in the evening my father woke. I said, "Forgive me if I hurt you. It had to be. But I am still and always will be your loyal son."

He said, as I remember, "You may be right. Perhaps it is true that we are pulling Frankland to bits. At least I know I have fathered a son who can look at a tasty sausage and say no." Seeing me wince a little he added, "And that may be what it is to be a man."

Now it came that Abbot Hugh of St Quentin, a much loved and respected man, last of the sons of the Great Charles and uncle to the reigning Charles, was killed. And of those who followed him many also died so that there was weeping and pain that need not have been. And the Count of Paris also was killed so that any oath to him was buried with his body, and the new Count, whom I met later, was less clever but more loyal.

And today I know who I am.

THE END